Working with Clodhopper

Mary Weeks Millard

© Day One Publications 2016

First printed 2016

ISBN 978-1-84625-516-8

All Scripture quotations are from the **New International Version** 1984
Copyright © 1973, 1978, 1984

Published by Day One Publications
Ryelands Road, Leominster, HR6 8NZ

TEL 01568 613 740 FAX 01568 611 473

email—sales@dayone.co.uk

UK web site—www.dayone.co.uk

Cover design by ELK Design

Printed by TJ International

Dedication

For Jake,

I am so glad that you enjoy my stories. May God bless you your whole life through.

Acknowledgements

My grateful thanks to the staff at Littlemoor Library who helped me research the lives of children in the Victorian era.

My grateful thanks to Tirzah Jones, Youth Director at DayOne Ministries and to Chris Jones for her careful editing of the manuscript.

As always, my grateful thanks to my husband Malcolm, for all his love, patience and support, without which I would not manage to write these books.

Chapter One

"Everything is going to change," announced Len Collins to his children one suppertime as they sat down to eat their lump of dry bread and have their bowl of thin soup.

Winifred and Wilfred looked up at their father. They were eleven year old twins. Some people called them Winnie and Will, but their mother had always called them 'my Two Freds'!

Everything had already changed for them since their mother had died a few weeks earlier. They looked at their father and wondered what was coming next. As usual, he was grumpy and seemed slightly drunk.

"I have made up my mind," he continued, "You will both leave school. We have no money and no food so, I am going to send you, Will, to the workhouse. They will feed you and no doubt get you some sort of apprenticeship—you are quite old enough to work. Winnie, I promised your mother that I would not send you to work in the mill. I must have been out of my mind, you could have made good money there, but I will keep my promise and so will find you some other job, probably in service as a maid. I can't afford to keep you at school any longer."

The Two Freds looked at each other in horror.

"But Pa," said Winnie, "you need us here. I can keep house just like I have done since Mam died and Will can get a job and still live at home!"

"I don't need you—you will be better away from here. Often I don't have any work and can't pay the rent. We could be turned out of the house at any time. I have made up my mind and that's that. Will, be ready to leave tomorrow morning. You only need the clothes you are wearing—you will be given workhouse clothes. Now finish eating and go to bed, both of you," growled their father.

The children did as they were told, too shocked to say anything. They knew it would be no use trying to argue, for once their father had made up his mind about something, they knew he wouldn't change it. Winnie took the bowls and plates into the scullery and washed them up. Will came out to help her. He put his arm around his sister's shoulder, trying to comfort her. How would they manage without each other? Even though they were now eleven they had done almost everything together, sharing their secrets and having adventures.

Soon they heard the door slam as their father went out.

"He'll be at the pub for a couple of hours now," commented Winnie, "At least we have this time together."

"No wonder we don't have money for food or rent," answered Will, "He doesn't do much work and spends all his wages in the ale house!"

"If only we could stay together we would manage somehow—we

both could have got some sort of work," said Winnie. "But now you have to go to the workhouse tomorrow and that's a horrible place! How will you manage?" she asked her brother, tearfully.

"Now come on Fred—be a man!" her brother replied. "You are older than I am, even if it is only by five minutes! We both have to stay strong. That's what Mam would have wanted."

"If only she hadn't caught consumption and died. I prayed so hard! Why did God let her die? She was such a lovely person. It doesn't seem fair," said Winnie, a tear trickling down her face.

"I know," replied Will. "I feel the same. Mam loved God so much too. At least she is in Heaven now and must be well and happy there. Pa can no longer beat or hurt her when he's drunk. Keep out of his way when he's been at the ale, Winnie, don't let him hurt you. I wish I could stay and take care of you always. When I am grown up I promise I will."

"I'll try," answered Winnie. "How can we keep in touch? How will I know that you are alright?"

"Do you know St. Cuthbert's church in town?" asked Will. "Every Sunday morning the workhouse children march to church there. Try to come along somehow and we at least can see each other and maybe pass a note to say how we are doing."

Winnie promised to do this. Both children knew enough about the workhouse to dread going there. It was the place where the poorest of the poor went and families were split up. The food was dreadful; barely enough to keep a person alive and everyone had to work very

7

hard for their keep. It was shameful that their father was sending Will to live there!

That night Winnie sobbed herself to sleep. How could she ever be happy again? First her lovely Mam had died and now her best mate, her twin brother, was being sent away! She hated her Pa!

Neither of them heard their father come in—drunk and disorderly—making a great deal of noise as he tried to put the key in the lock and then falling asleep sitting at the table.

Chapter Two

Next morning Winnie woke to the sun streaming in the window. Any other day she would have been happy at the prospect of a sunny day and would have joined the birds as they sang their dawn chorus. However, her heart was too heavy to enjoy the sunshine or the birds because she knew she would be saying goodbye to her twin brother and also leaving school. She sighed deeply as she got up and dressed. There was no indoor toilet or bathroom in the small terraced house where the family lived. She had to go through the back door down to the bottom of the garden to the outhouse. At least in Coronation Street where they lived, each house had its own privy (as the toilet was called). In many of the streets around them several families had to share the same one!

Their little red brick house had two main rooms upstairs, one had been her parent's room, but her father rarely bothered to go upstairs to sleep anymore, so Will had taken to using it. Then Winnie slept in the smaller bedroom. Before her mother had died, she and Will used to share it. There was also one very tiny room—more like a cupboard, which her mother had called the 'box room'. It was used to store everything from old clothes to old furniture and even the pram they had used as babies! Downstairs there were also two main rooms. At the front was a sitting room, called the parlour and was only used on Sundays or when visitors came. It had been her mother's pride and joy and was always kept polished and tidy. The back room was a dining room where all the family lived and ate their meals. It had a table and a set of four hard chairs, a rocking chair near the black range which served both as a fire and also as a cooker. Leading off the back room was a kitchen—not like our modern kitchens, but it had a stone floor and a sink where the family washed everything, themselves, their clothes and their pots and pans! A large cupboard housed all the pots, pans, brooms and cleaning materials and a row of shelves held most of the food. Of course, since there were no fridges or freezers, fresh food was bought each day.

Winnie stoked the fire and filled the kettle ready to make some porridge and tea. By now her dad was stirring and began to call up the stairs to Will.

"Soon as you 'ave had your porridge we'll be off—so 'urry up, lad."

Winnie heard Will's boots stomping down the stairs—quite slowly. She knew he didn't want to go. Normally, he ran down the stairs at top speed. She hardly dared look at his face; she didn't want to cry and make things worse for him.

"And you, my maid, get up to that school and tell the teacher that you both are leaving for good!" said her father.

"Can I stay at school today, Pa?" Winnie asked.

Her father hesitated a minute, then answered, "Alright, but this is the last day. You've had enough learning now in order to get a job. If we can't get you one quickly, then you'll 'ave to go to the workhouse too."

They ate their breakfast in silence. It didn't take long—there was so little to eat! Will gave his sister a hug and took his cap off the peg and followed his father out of the door.

Trying not to cry, Winnie cleared the dishes and washed them up. Then she went upstairs to tidy the bedrooms. There was just time to do that before school. She didn't want to be late—she didn't want to miss one minute of her last day. She loved school and she and Will were the best students in the juniors and everyone knew they could have won scholarships to the grammar school if they had the chance.

Sadly, Winnie tidied up her brother's clothes. She hated to think he would now wear workhouse uniform! Knowing her Pa would sell all Will's clothes, she suddenly decided to keep a set in her room under her mattress. It would seem as if her twin were still near her. Maybe a miracle would happen and he could somehow come back home and then he would still have some clothes!

Winnie had to run all the way up Coronation Street and then two other streets to reach the school. The bell rang as she arrived and rather breathlessly she joined the queue to march into the classroom. They had to march in silence, so she couldn't tell her best friend, Madge, that this was to be her last day. In fact, she had to wait until play time to tell both her teacher and her friends. Her teacher looked at her sadly as Winnie told her about Will being taken to the workhouse and that she was to go into service.

Will tried to be brave as he walked alongside his father. Everyone dreaded going to the workhouse. It is what people did when they had no hope, nothing left in life. He felt as if he was being discarded by his father because he was not wanted, he was just another mouth to feed and there was no money and no food.

"If only Mam was still alive," he thought to himself, "she would never have allowed this to happen to her Two Freds."

They arrived at the large stone building. It looked grim—more like a prison than a home. There were lots of small windows with bars across them and tall iron railings outside. His father rang the bell. It clanged loudly and Will shivered, partly with fright and partly because he felt so ashamed at having to enter a workhouse.

A rather elderly shrivelled-up man opened the door and glowered at them.

"What do you want?" he asked Will's father.

"I want my son admitted. I have no wife, no money and can't feed or clothe him any longer," he answered.

"Best come on in," the man said, frowning at Will. "I'll get the Master."

Will and his father were taken into a dingy office where a man was sitting at a desk writing in a large book. He looked up when they were brought in by the porter.

"What is your business?" he asked gruffly. "And make it quick, I am very busy!"

Will's father explained once again that he wanted his son to be admitted. The man put down his pen and listened to the sorry tale of woe. In fact, Will thought his Pa was making things at home sound ten times worse than they really were. "He just wants rid of me," he thought to himself sadly.

Within minutes, all Will's details were written down in the large book and his father was dismissed. The Master rang a bell and the porter appeared again.

"Take this boy to the Matron of the boys' dormitory and tell her to admit him," he said in his gruff voice; then to Will, "We run a strict house here, anyone who breaks the rules is punished severely. Remember that!"

"Yes sir," answered Will, his heart sinking into his boots as he followed the porter through what seemed like endless corridors to the wing kept for the boys. He knew that families were separated in the workhouse with men, women, small children under ten years, older boys and girls all kept apart.

Finally, they reached the boys' wing. It was very quiet and Will wondered where all the boys were. He was taken to the Matron, who looked him up and down.

"What's your name, boy?" Will was asked.

"Wilfred Collins, ma'am," he replied quietly.

"Speak up, don't mumble. I don't like boys who mumble," she said sharply. She was a tall, skinny woman, with a long nose and she looked down her nose at Will. Will somehow thought that she didn't like boys, full stop. He repeated his name speaking clearly and quite loudly.

"Don't shout at me! I'm not deaf! Wilfred, you said. I expect you'll get called Fred here. Well, Fred, take off all your clothes and let me look at you."

Will was horrified. Nobody except his Mam had called him Fred—that was her pet name for her twins, the 'Two Freds'. The thought that these strangers would call him by that name was awful! Then, to have to undress completely in front of a strange woman was humiliating. However, Will had no choice. His clothes were dropped in a pile and he shivered with both cold and embarrassment as the matron examined him. He felt like an insect on the floor, not a person at all. She was looking for infestations like scabies and lice—but even though they were poor, the twins had always been kept clean. Their Mam had been very particular about cleanliness. She always said it was next to godliness. Having been examined, the Matron then shaved Will's head with a razor. She said it was to stop him catching head lice. Once again, poor Will felt humiliated.

Eventually, his ordeal was over and he was given a package of clothes and told to dress himself. He folded his own clothes and the woman tied them into a bundle with string and put a label with his name on them.

"You'll be given those back again when you leave—if you ever do," she said meanly.

"Now come with me," Matron continued. "The boys are all in school. It's school in the morning, work in the afternoon and evening. You'll soon get used to the routine. The timetable is on the wall in the dormitory. I will take you and show you where you will sleep. I hope you are not a bed-wetter. If you are, you have to wash your own sheets in the morning. You'll soon learn our ways."

Will was shown a bed at the end of a long line. There was a window above it, but far too high for him to look out. He felt like he was in prison. His mind was in a whirl. Why did his Pa hate him so much that he sent him here? Why couldn't he have lived at home and gone out to work? What had happened to his Pa since his Mam had become ill and died? Before then he used to be a happy man and go out to work and not spend his time or his money in the pub getting drunk.

Chapter Three

The house seemed so deserted when Winnie returned from school. She went upstairs to her room and tried to keep herself busy by tidying up her few belongings. She made sure that Will's clothes were well hidden under her mattress, then took from a cupboard her one special possession. It was a tin which her mother had given her just before she died. Carefully, Winnie took off the lid and handled the precious items which were inside. In an envelope was her birth certificate and also Will's. It was strange that her father didn't come looking for that before he took Will away. Maybe he had forgotten about it because birth certificates had been introduced soon after they were born. She had promised her Mam to keep these things safe and not let her father get hold of them. Another envelope had some money inside, which was for emergencies. There were some very pretty pieces of jewellery as well, wrapped in a handkerchief on which the letters E.M.E. had been interwoven by embroidery. There was also a very small, black leather Bible. Winnie loved the feel of the leather as she stroked her hand over it and the leathery smell was lovely too. It reminded her of her Mam who used to read from it every day. When she became too sick to be able to read it herself, Winnie or Will read to her after school. Her Mam had given it to her and told her to read it every day for it was the most precious book in the whole, wide world. Winnie loved to look at the Bible, but the print was very small and she hadn't yet begun to read it for herself.

Carefully, Winnie packed her treasures away for she knew her father would soon be back.

What was she supposed to do all day long since she was not allowed to go to school? Maybe she should start to scrub the doorstep like her Mam had done when she was well. If her Pa saw she was busy, perhaps he wouldn't send her out to work as a servant but let her stay at home and look after the house.

The step was almost finished when her father returned. He had no smile for his daughter, though he did take care as he stepped over the wet doorstep.

"Is Will alright?" she couldn't help asking. Her Pa just nodded and gave a grunt.

"I need a cup of tea and then I'm going out to look for work. Maybe someone will give me work clearing up in the market. I'll be back at six for my tea," he said.

"I hope you get some work, Pa," Winnie answered, "because the housekeeping tin is almost empty—we need food."

"Alright, don't tell me what to do young lady. The sooner we get you a job the better. We'll talk about that tonight," he said crossly.

Once he had finished his tea he went out, slamming the door behind him. Winnie sat in the rocking chair and began to cry. What was she going to do? What would happen to her?

Winnie spent the rest of the afternoon spring cleaning the house. It made her feel better to work hard and make things look nicer. Her Mam had always kept everything clean and tidy and had been proud of their little house. Once the housework was finished Winnie took the basket and the last penny from the housekeeping tin and went out to the shops. In those days the shops stayed open well into the evening. The butcher was a big man who always seemed to be cheerful and gave Winnie a smile when she walked into his shop.

"Well, here's a sight to cheer a man's heart," he said. "What can I do for this pretty lass?"

"Have you got two small pieces of liver?" she asked politely.

"Only two today, Winnie?" the butcher looked at her. "Who is going without their tea? Someone been naughty in your house and going to bed without any supper?" he said in fun.

"Oh no, it's not like that," replied Winnie, with a tear trickling down her face. "Our Will has been taken to the workhouse and soon I'm to be sent away into service."

"I'm so sorry, dear," said the kindly butcher. "I didn't mean to upset you. Things have been bad for you all since your poor mother died. Let me get that liver for you."

He cut two small slices of liver and wrapped them in paper, then added a sausage and a slice of bacon as well. "That's a little gift from me," he added, taking only a farthing for the liver and handing her three farthings in change from the penny she handed him.

"Thank you so much, you are so kind," Winnie said with a smile as she went to the greengrocer's shop to buy two potatoes and then to the grocer to get some stale bread. At least tonight they would not go to bed hungry. Maybe that would put her Pa into a better mood.

At the workhouse, Will was taken into the classroom. The teacher was not happy at being interrupted and glowered at his new pupil.

"Sit at that bench," he said, pointing his cane in the direction of the back row where three boys were already squashed together. Will did as he was told, the boys squeezing up to make room.

"His name is Fred," Matron told the teacher. "He's eleven and healthy."

At least the lessons were easy! All the questions he was asked by the teacher he was able to answer and when called out to read from the book which they were using for English, he had no problems. For the first time that day, someone smiled at him.

"Not bad, Fred. Not bad at all. Maybe at last I have got a scholar among you lot of dimwits," he told the class.

After school had finished the boys crowded round Will.

"Who are you then, teacher's pet?" sneered one big lad. "We'll soon make you sorry that you know so much!"

"Fred, Fred, too many brains in his head," chanted another boy and then everyone seemed to take it up and the whole room rang with their taunts.

Only one lad, who was much smaller and had metal braces around his legs, stood up for him.

"Shut up, you lot, or we'll have Matron beating us all for being too noisy! Leave the lad alone and let him get used to this 'orrible place."

After a lunch that consisted of thin cabbage soup and a lump of stale bread, the boys were sent out into a playground for an hour. Leapfrog was one of the most popular games and since Will had a strong back, he was included. He felt sorry for the boy who had stood up for him because he wasn't able to join in and just stood around most of the time. After a while, Will left the game and went to talk with the boy. He asked him his name and learnt he was called Eric and was also eleven, but because he had deformed legs, he was small for his age.

"Have you been here long?" Will asked him, telling him that really he was called Wilfred and usually called Will by his friends.

"I've lived here all my life, or as long as I can remember," Eric told him. "My mother died giving birth to me and I don't know about my father. It's alright so long as you do what you're told and don't wet the bed. Heaven help you if you are a bed-wetter!" he warned Will.

"Thank you for standing up for me after school," said Will. "I can't help it if I learn easily. My twin sister and I were always top of our classes."

"Don't let them get you down. You have to stand up for yourself here. Some of those boys are bullies, but it's because we are all bullied by the staff. They know no better."

By the end of the day, Will knew that he had made a new friend in Eric and somehow that made things just a little more bearable.

When he was getting ready for bed in the long, cold dormitory, he found he was sleeping next to Eric and was able to help him take the irons off his legs and get into his nightshirt.

"One day I'll get out of this place and then take care of Winnie," he promised himself as he fell asleep from exhaustion.

Chapter Four

That evening, Winnie did her very best to make a really nice meal for her Pa. She was quite a good cook, even though she was only eleven because her mother had taught her when she first became unwell. In fact, Winnie really enjoyed cooking, though she didn't like looking after the old black cooking range so much! It needed a lot of raking out and keeping clean inside as well as polishing and blacking the outside.

Her father seemed to be in quite a good mood when he arrived home. He had done some casual work in the market clearing up and earned a little money. He had also been given some over-ripe fruit and vegetables. He dropped a couple of coins into the housekeeping tin and Winnie stored the food in the kitchen. She knew she could make some soup with the veggies and maybe stew the fruit with a little sugar.

They sat down to eat the meal together and Winnie served her Pa with the sausage and bacon along with his slice of liver. He even smiled at his daughter.

"Well, this is good!" he complimented her. "We should be able to get you into service without any trouble. Your Mam trained you well!" he added.

Winnie tried to smile and not to say anything which might anger him.

"I'm going down to The Cock and Hen to see my friends, but when I come home we must talk about your future."

"Alright," replied Winnie. "But Sunday morning, please may I go to church, like I used to with Mam?"

Winnie had decided it was best to ask her Pa while he was in a good mood and before he went out drinking.

"Don't see why not," he answered, "but be home in time to make me my dinner. You're a good lass. Sorry I had to send Will away, but it's for the best."

Winnie swallowed back her tears. She knew her Pa would hate her to cry and she began to clear away the dishes. Soon she heard the door bang and gave a sigh of relief. Even though it was lonely on her own, lately, she had become scared of her father when he came home after a drinking bout. Will had always been there to protect her, but now she was on her own.

When all the household jobs were finished, Winnie lit a candle and decided that maybe she should read from the Bible her mother had given her. She went upstairs to her bedroom and took it out of the tin. It was hard to read the tiny print by candlelight, but she turned to her mother's favourite psalm, number 23. She read it slowly, thinking about the words.

This is what it said, but in more modern English:

The Lord is my shepherd, I shall lack nothing.

He makes me lie down in green pastures, he leads me beside quiet waters,

He restores my soul. He guides me in paths of righteousness for his name's sake.

Even though I walk through the valley of the shadow of death, I will fear no

evil, for you are with me; your rod and your staff they comfort me.

You prepare a table before me in the presence of my enemies.

You anoint my head with oil; my cup overflows.

Surely goodness and love will follow me all the days of my life,

And I will dwell in the house of the Lord for ever.

Although Winnie didn't understand what all the words meant, she felt peaceful after reading it. Her Mam had told her to pray to Jesus, the Good Shepherd, not just when she needed help, but at all times. So far she hadn't bothered, but now she wanted to. She really, really wanted to talk to someone and know she wasn't on her own, so she closed her eyes and asked Jesus to help her and to keep her safe. Then Winnie blew out the candle and went to sleep.

An hour or two afterwards, she was woken by a noise. She was used to her Pa coming in at night, but she could hear voices talking together. What was going on? Could it be burglars? After a few minutes Winnie decided to light her candle again and she crept down the stairs, her heart beating so loudly she was sure the people in the back room must be able to hear it! As she got nearer to the door, she could hear that one of the men was her Pa. The other voice she recognised as belonging to the pub landlord. He had never been to the house before. Winnie didn't like him at all. He was older than her Pa and had a lot of children who ran around the place and were dirty and uncared for. Winnie sometimes felt sorry for them, especially when their mother had died with influenza.

"She's eleven, you say?" asked the landlord. "A good age. A pretty lass as I remember and clever with it."

"Oh yes," she heard her Pa reply, "both of my children are clever, clever with numbers and reading. She's good at cooking too. You should 'ave seen the tea I had this evening! She keeps the 'ouse lovely too. My Winnie's a gem!"

"Well mate, I reckon that's settled. I'll take 'er. She can take care of me 'ouse and 'ome; do the books for the pub; serve at the bar and in a little while maybe she can become me wife!"

Winnie gasped, almost so loudly she was afraid her Pa would find her on the bottom stair. It looked as if he was doing some sort of bargain to sell her to that awful man! She would rather have gone to the mill and worked! If only her Mam hadn't made her Pa promise that she would never be sent to work in the mill! This was a much worse fate. What could she do?

"You tell 'er tomorrow and send 'er to me on Monday morning and I'll pay you 'er wages every week. Then you can pay off what you owe me! You'll even see 'er when you come for a drink!" the landlord said with a nasty laugh.

Winnie shuddered. She had heard enough! Very quietly she climbed back up the stairs, being careful not to step on the creaky parts of the stair, and slipped back into her bedroom.

Part of her felt very, very angry and part of her hated her Pa. How could he do this to her?

She lay awake trying to think what to do. How could she escape? She would rather have been sent to the workhouse like Will than to be sent to work for the landlord of The Cock and Hen.

When her anger had died down a bit she thought again about Jesus the Good Shepherd. Her Mam had told her often that he loved children. Each one was a special lamb. How could he love her when he allowed things like this to go on? Nobody who loved children would let such bad things happen!

She turned over and tried to sleep. She would have to make a plan in the morning.

She thought about Will and began to cry. That night Winnie cried herself to sleep.

Saturday dragged by very slowly as Winnie tried to occupy herself around the house. She missed Will so much! All the time she dreaded her father wanting to talk to her about starting work on Monday, but he went back to the market to work and then to the pub in the evening.

On Sunday she got up as usual and went downstairs to find her Pa asleep in the chair. As quietly as she could she raked out the ashes and re-lit the fire, ready to make porridge and tea for their breakfast. She prepared some vegetables and put them on the stove to cook slowly for the soup. While she was doing this an idea came to her. The first thing she had to do was to get a note to Will. When they were smaller they had devised a secret code, so that they could give each other messages which no one else could read. It had been a fun thing to do. The messages had never been very important. Now she had to write a really important message to Will and it had to be in code so that if by any chance it fell into the wrong hands, then no one else would be able to read or understand it.

Upstairs in Will's room was his old exercise book. She had kept it to tear out the pages and hang up to use in the privy (toilet). Winnie knew there were a few blank pages at the end of the book, so she tore one out and with her pencil began to compose the message.

HWVL EXRR,

JV MVOM X SZMN SVLLO DXM SVNW MVS. X VS LZTTXTC VEVO. X EXRR ELXNW EDWT X GVT. EXND RYAW, EXTTXW.

When she had finished she carefully folded the message and put it into her pocket. Somehow, she would get that letter to the workhouse!

Her Pa began to stir and call for her.

"Winnie, where the dickens are you?" he yelled.

She quickly ran downstairs and said brightly,

"Breakfast is ready, Pa. Do you want to go and wash first or shall I put it on the table?"

"I'll have it now," he answered, "and don't come home late from that church or wherever you said you were going. I have good news for you. Yes, very good news! You can start work tomorrow!"

"Tomorrow? So soon?" Winnie tried to make herself sound surprised. "I'll be off now, Pa. See you when I get back and you can tell me all about it."

As quickly as she could Winnie wrapped her thin shawl around her shoulders and ran out of the house, holding the important letter which was in her pocket.

"Good Shepherd, please help me to get it to Will," she prayed silently as she walked towards the workhouse, wondering what time the children would march to the church.

Chapter Five

Winnie stood under a tree on the road near the church. It was in the centre of the town and she didn't want to draw attention to herself. She had a rough idea of the time of day—of course she had no watch, but the bells in the steeple had just started to ring to call people to church, so she knew she wasn't too late.

After a few minutes she saw a crocodile of girls walking along the road, all dressed in the same workhouse uniform dresses and bonnets. Once they had passed, after a few more minutes the boys appeared. Winnie became very excited. She was sure that Will would be on the lookout for her, so she stepped out from the shadow of the tree and waited. It was a long crocodile of lads—and she peered among the ranks looking for Will but then became worried because there was no sign of him. Then, at the very back she saw him. He was alongside a boy who was struggling to walk and keep up with everybody because he had iron bars each side of his legs to support them. Today we would call them callipers. As they came near to Winnie, the boy stumbled and fell and Will went at once to help him. This gave Winnie the opportunity she needed. She ran over to help the lad, giving Will a grin and passing the note to him. She was pretty sure that the Master who was walking behind the boys, didn't see anything and she dared not speak in case Will got into trouble as the

Master looked very fierce and instead of helping the poor boy who had fallen, was scolding him and Will and telling them to hurry up. He turned to Winnie and said a curt 'Thank you, but we don't need your help', then turned to Will and said, "Get a move on, Fred. Eric can manage well without you. He did before you came to us and will continue to do so."

"Yes, sir," Will answered the Master and even in his voice Winnie could hear his unhappiness.

Winnie ran away quickly and entered the church, looking around for somewhere where she could sit. A hand touched her arm and she turned quickly. To her joy it was her school friend Madge sitting with her family.

"Come and sit with us," whispered Madge, then looking at her mother asked, "That's alright, isn't it, Mam?"

"Of course, dear," replied Madge's mother and they all squeezed along the pew to allow Winnie to join them. The boys soon filed into the church and as they took off their caps, to her horror Winnie saw that they all had shaved heads. She looked for Will, but because they all wore the same clothes and had no hair it took her a while to locate her brother, but once she had, she hardly took her eyes off him. When would she see him again? It was hard to concentrate on the service and it had been so long since she had attended church with her Mam that she found it hard to find the right places in the prayer book, but Madge helped her. She did remember one thing which the minister said in his sermon. He looked over to the children of the workhouse and smiled at them.

"We must all remember," he said, "however difficult our lives may seem, that God is our loving Father. He knows each one of us by name and loves us all. We can pray to him at any time and anywhere."

Somehow, it comforted Winnie to know that the minister cared about the workhouse children and maybe if he smiled at them each week, it would comfort Will.

She had been shocked to hear the Master call Will 'Fred'. Only their mother had ever used that pet name for her two children, but as she thought about it a sudden idea came to her. She would be 'Fred' too! If she was going to run away that afternoon, she had to change who she was so that no one would recognise her. She had Will's clothes under her mattress. They would only be a little bit too big for her. She would cut off her long hair and wear Will's cap. She would pretend to be a boy! That way she would be safer and more likely to get some work. It seemed a brilliant idea and at the close of the service when everyone knelt to pray she asked Jesus to help her escape safely.

When the service was over the workhouse children all marched out and as the boys filed past the pew where she still sat with Madge's family, Will gave her a wink. She knew it wasn't at all ladylike, but she winked back. Anyway, she had to practise being a boy from now on!

Madge's Mam talked to her for a few minutes, saying how sorry she was that Winnie had to leave school and told her that she could always come and visit Madge when she was free. Winnie thanked her nicely and said goodbye to her friend, explaining that her Pa was expecting her home and tomorrow she was to start work somewhere as a maid.

"Where will that be?" asked Madge.

"My Pa hasn't yet told me," she answered truthfully, glad she didn't have to tell her friend a lie. "I don't think I will be very free from now on. I wish I could have stayed on at school, but everything has changed. Did you see Will in that crocodile of workhouse lads? He was the one sitting by the boy who can't walk properly. At least I can see him when I come to church!"

Madge squeezed her hand. "You'll always be my best friend. I won't forget you or Will and will pray for you at bedtime."

"Thank you," said Winnie, tears in her eyes. "I'll never forget you either."

Then Winnie pulled her shawl around her shoulders and left the church. The minister shook her hand and smiled at her and she thought he must really like children.

"I must remember what he told us about being loved by God even if things are hard," she thought to herself as she hurried through the town to get her Pa's dinner ready.

Her Pa was indoors, looking unhappy as he always did these days.

"I saw Will," Winnie told him, trying to act as normally as possible. "He was helping another boy who had his legs in irons and couldn't walk properly."

Her Pa grunted, then looked up at his daughter. "Well, he's alright then. Good. Now about tomorrow," he hesitated a little, then added,

"You are to start work at The Cock and Hen; you will live on the premises and look after the children, be housekeeper and also help with keeping the books—you know, the adding up of the money and that sort of thing. You'll be one of the family, so to speak, and I don't doubt that I'll see you sometimes."

"But Pa," began Winnie, but her father interrupted.

"Don't 'Pa' me," he said fiercely. "Tomorrow at nine sharp you will be there, and make sure you leave your room tidy because I may take in a lodger."

"Yes, Pa," Winnie said quietly, not daring to look at him. Thank goodness she had a plan of escape!

Chapter Six

S oon after this conversation with her Pa, Winnie heard him go out.

"I'll not be back until around six o'clock for my tea," he shouted, as he banged the door. As soon as the coast was clear, Winnie started to put her plan into action. She knew that she had to get as far away as she could as quickly as possible. She rushed upstairs and pulled out Will's clothes from under her mattress. Then she went to her cupboard and gathered together her precious tin of special treasures and also a few other items she thought she might need. She went down to the front parlour and took the largest pair of scissors she could find from her Mam's sewing basket. She decided that maybe some needles and thread might also come in useful so she added these to her pile of belongings and then took them all down to the privy at the bottom of the garden.

It took all her courage to undertake the next task. With the scissors she cut off her lovely long hair. It made her cry a little as she did it. What would her Mam have said? Winnie knew the reason why her Mam had made her Pa promise never to send her to the mill to work was because one day while her mother was working at the loom a terrible accident had happened and a little girl's hair became caught in the machinery. The injuries had been horrific and eventually the girl had died. After that incident she was afraid for all the young girls who worked in the mill that even though they wore bonnets to keep their hair out of the way, such an accident might happen again. The small girls were often sent under the machines to join up broken threads and were put into great danger by doing that.

Once her hair was short, Winnie changed into Will's clothing and covered her head with his old cap. She felt very funny and just hoped that she now looked like a boy. Acting as a boy, she would have a better chance of getting some work and be not so easily recognised if the police were looking for a missing girl. She bundled her old clothes and hair together in her shawl, hoping to throw them into the canal once she was a good way from home. Then, all her other belongings were tied into a sheet. Winnie ran out of the back gate and down the alley which ran between Coronation Street and the next road. Instead of heading into the small town where she might possibly be recognised, she ran in the opposite direction towards the Leeds and Liverpool canal. Having reached the canal Winnie began to walk along the tow path in the direction of the market town of Skipton. It was a busy town and she thought she might find it easier to get lost in the crowds there.

Winnie and Will had always loved the canal, enjoying the busyness of the narrow boats being pulled up and down by the large horses. Some of the boats were brightly painted with roses and the boat men and women wore a sort of uniform. Everyone seemed friendly and they helped each other to work the many locks on the canal.

Nobody seemed to take any notice of Winnie as she walked down the tow path. Every now and then she had to be careful as she overtook a horse, pulling its heavy burden along the water way. Soon her feet felt very sore and she knew she must have blisters. She was wearing Will's socks and shoes and they were really too big for her, but if she wore her own boots it would have been a certain giveaway, for only girls wore long boots with lots of buttons.

In the end, her walking was becoming so slow that she decided to take off her shoes and socks. She stuffed the socks into her trouser pockets and tied the laces of the shoes together and hung them around her neck. It was much better to walk in bare feet. Winnie was quite used to doing that, anyway. Through the summer months she and most of her friends went without shoes.

It was a lovely March day, cool, but sunny. A few early primroses and violets were in the bank near the tow path and Winnie would have just loved to have picked some. How much her Mam had loved the smell of wild violets!

Winnie walked on for some miles. She was beginning to get very tired and the light was fading. Where would she spend the night? Any time now her Pa would return home and find she had run away. Had she gone far enough to be safe? Winnie didn't feel at all safe! If her Pa had been out drinking (and she guessed he had) and if he was angry, then he could become violent. Often her Mam had been hit by him and she knew that he wouldn't hesitate to beat her if he found her.

It was almost dark when Winnie came to an inn just by the tow path. Several horses were tied up outside and there was a pump and a trough full of water for them. Winnie was so thirsty that she put down her two bundles and scooped up some of the water to have a drink. It tasted so cool and sweet.

"Hey laddie, that's not good water for you. I'll get you some fresh from the pump!" boomed a loud voice. It made Winnie jump! She almost forgot she was dressed as a lad. She turned round to see a large man, dressed in a waistcoat and flat cap looking down at her. He smiled nicely and so she felt slightly less worried.

"Thank you sir. That would be very nice," she answered politely.

Having had a long drink from a tin cup which the man held out to her, he asked her,

"You look like you are on a trip. Where are you heading?"

"Not quite sure, sir," she answered. "Sort of heading out towards Liverpool. I'm hoping to get some work. I've just left school."

"Well, laddie," the boater said, looking Winnie up and down, "you're not very big, but maybe you are stronger than you look. My missus and I could use a hand on the boat, especially going through the Foulridge Tunnel. Our youngsters have all left 'ome now and the missus hasn't been so good of late. You'll have to work 'ard, but I'll be fair with you and there'll be proper meals thrown in. The missus is a real good cook! Pick up yer bundle and come over to our boat and let's see what she thinks. You'd best tell me yer name."

"Fred, sir," Winnie replied without hesitation. "Fred Collins."

"Come on then, Fred. And you had better leave off calling me 'sir' all the time. Plain Dan will do and the missus is Mabel. Dan and

Mabel Potter and this is our horse, Clodhopper," he said, untying a large grey horse and leading them both over to a barge which had 'Bright Water' painted on the side.

The narrow boat looked inviting. A lamp shone out of one of the windows and the boat had roses painted on its sides. It somehow looked like a home which was loved. Scared, but also a little excited, Winnie walked over the narrow plank from the canal bank into the back of the boat. Dan tied Clodhopper to a large iron post to which the boat was also secured by a very thick rope. There was a lovely smell of stew as Winnie entered the boat and she realised that she was very hungry. She also felt that in a strange way she had come to a safe place where her Pa wouldn't find her. Maybe the Good Shepherd was looking after her.

Chapter Seven

"Come and see our new helper," Dan shouted to Mabel as they entered the barge. A large woman came to the door of the living quarters and beamed at Winnie with a welcoming smile.

"Welcome," she said. "We could certainly do with some help around here!"

"I'm Fred Collins—at your service!" said Winnie, remembering to remove her cap, as she understood that a polite young boy would have been taught to do so. It was still very strange to have short hair!

Mabel looked at Winnie, paused for a moment and then smiled again.

"Well, supper is about ready and now I have two hungry men to feed! Come in, come in, I'll show you round—not that's there's much to see in our tiny home!"

A major worry was springing into Winnie's mind. Where would she sleep and wash and things like that? How could she keep her secret that she was a girl and not a boy?

It certainly was very cramped in the living quarters of the boat. There was a sitting area with a stove in the middle that belched out a lot of smoke. It made Winnie's eyes water and took her a time to be able to see things clearly. There were a couple of chairs, a couch and a foldaway table. Then there was a tiny area curtained off which had a wash stand and bowl and a bucket with a lid, which by the smell she knew was used as a toilet. Mabel showed her the facilities and also told her that from time to time they stopped off at places where they were able to visit the public baths and washhouses.

At the far end of the living area a step led up to a tiny bedroom.

"This is where Dan and I sleep," she explained, "Will you be comfortable sleeping on the couch? Our children all did that and liked it as it was warm in the winter. In the summer sometimes, they slept up on the roof on a mattress.

"I'd love to do that!" Winnie exclaimed. "It would be so exciting to sleep under the stars!"

Dan, who had followed her inside, let out a deep chuckle. "It's fine, my lad, until it rains!"

Winnie was very grateful that the old couple didn't ask her too many questions as they all tucked into their supper. She told them that she was eleven years old and had just left school and that her Mam had recently died from a disease called consumption. She didn't want to lie to these kind people who had offered her a home and job. Pretending to be a boy was bad enough!

After supper Dan explained about some of the jobs with which he wanted her to help. She would take care of Clodhopper, except when they went through tunnels. In the tunnels he would like her to help with 'legging' but needed to know her legs were both long enough and strong enough to do that. Mabel found it too difficult now and so would lead Clodhopper over the tunnel and meet them when they came out the other side. He also wanted help with working the locks, loading cargo, collecting kindling wood for the fire, emptying the 'toilet' and fetching water.

Winnie thought she would be able to manage these things easily.

"I can also help with the dishes and even cooking," she told Mabel, "I had to help a lot when my Mam was sick."

"Now, Fred," Dan continued, "I'll put your wages each week in this tin," and he pointed to a tin on the shelf of the living area. You can take money from it and use it when you want to do so, but Mabel will provide all your meals. There are very few places with shops along the tow path, so I suggest you save it until you reach Liverpool. When we get there, you can decide if you want to stay with us on the boat and we can decide if we want you to stay! Otherwise, we can go our separate ways. Is that agreed?"

"Yes, Dan, and thank you very much," answered Winnie and they shook hands on the agreement. It made her feel very grown up and quite excited about being out at work!

After they had eaten and cleared away the dishes, Mabel informed Winnie that it was now bedtime for them all as they had to get up early each morning and start on their way. If they were too late, then they had to queue a long time to get through the locks and check in at the various canal company offices en route. They always tried to be ahead of schedule because if they arrived early in Liverpool with their cargo, then they could all earn a bonus.

"Before bed, we always say a few prayers together," Dan told her. "You are an answer to our prayers, laddie, even last night we asked our Father in heaven to send us some help. That's why I wasn't afraid to ask you to work with us, for I am sure you have been sent by God. Do you say your prayers, Fred?"

"Not always," answered Winnie, truthfully, "but Mam left me her Bible and I have been reading the Shepherd psalm which she loved and I did ask the Good Shepherd to keep me safe and help me find a job and somewhere to live."

"I think we will get on just fine," beamed Mabel. "Neither Dan nor I can read or write. We never went to school. We'd love it if you were sometimes to read us a bit from the Bible. We can all learn more about God together!"

Winnie went to her bundle and found her Bible. It was a bit hard to see in the smoky room and by paraffin lamp, but she found Psalm 23 and read it out loud to the couple. Then Dan said a prayer, thanking God for sending Fred to them and asking for a safe night and that all their loved ones would be blessed. Winnie said a loud 'amen', thinking so much of Will and hoping that he too would be safe and happy.

She didn't undress, for she had no boy's nightshirt to wear, but curled up on the couch and fell sound asleep.

Next morning at first light she woke to hear Mabel stoking the fire and quickly she got up to help. Then she took Clodhopper his oats and went to the pump at the inn to get water and to empty the bucket at the Inn's privy. She was amazed to find that, not only was it indoors, but it also had a chain to pull and water fell down from a cistern above it. Winnie had never seen anything so modern, although her teacher had told the class about such new inventions.

At the pump she quickly washed her face and hands and after a bowl of porridge, Dan, Mabel and Winnie were ready to set off.

"You hold Clodhopper's reins and lead her along the tow path," instructed Dan. "When we reach the first lock, I will show you how to help the lock keeper to open the gates."

So, the first working day of her life began, and it wasn't working for the landlord of The Cock and Hen. Winnie did wonder what Will was doing and also what her Pa was thinking. Were the police on the lookout for her? She would have to be careful! The sooner they got on their way the better!

Chapter Eight

On the Sunday afternoon when Winnie ran away from home, her father, Len Collins was feeling terrible. He felt so angry with himself because of the way he was behaving; angry at God because his dear wife had died; angry at the world in general because nothing seemed to ever go his way. The only way he knew to help him to forget his anger and feel better was to drown his sorrows drinking ale, so as usual he took himself to The Cock and Hen.

The landlord filled his pewter tankard with ale and gave him a twisted sort of smile.

"I'll have little Winnie to cheer me up tomorrow!" he said, giving Len a wink.

Len didn't answer. He felt so bad about almost selling his daughter into nothing less than slavery—he knew it would be a bad life for her—but he needed the money and the goodwill of the landlord to pay for his drinking habits.

He thought back over his life. Len could barely read or write—he'd had very little schooling and when he did attend school he was far more interested in playing conkers or kicking a ball around than he was about learning anything useful. When he left school as a boy of eight, he became a labourer, getting any unskilled work he could find. Often it was farm labouring, for he enjoyed being outdoors. One day, when he was about twenty years old working on an estate farm cutting corn, he saw a beautiful girl bringing refreshments to the workers in the fields. She was gorgeous and he decided then and there, impossible as it might seem, that he would marry her!

Len later learned that the girl was none other than Ernestina Mountjoy Evans, the daughter of the squire. They lived in the manor house and it was on their land that the harvest was being gathered.

At that time Len was a very handsome young man and so caught the eye of all the girls as he travelled from place to place finding work. He also caught the eye of Tina, as Ernestina was nicknamed. She was bored with her life and longing for adventure, so when it appeared in the shape of Len, she felt very excited. At the Harvest Supper which the squire gave to all the farm workers, she got to know Len a little more and then they danced together at the barn dance which followed. Over the next couple of weeks Tina met up with Len in the evenings and they quickly fell in love. Tina knew there was no way that her father would allow her to marry a farm labourer, so one night she gathered a few belongings together and the couple eloped (running away to get married). It seemed such a huge adventure at the time! They managed to travel hitching lifts on farm carts, all the way to Gretna Green, where they then got married, which was so romantic.

Len sighed as he remembered those days! He and Tina had been so happy together. They had settled in a Lancashire mill town where she had found work in a cotton mill and he found work wherever he could. He had always worried that she would miss her family, friends and all the luxuries which she was used to enjoying. Her new life was very hard and the small home which they rented could not have been more different than the beautiful mansion where she had grown up. However, Tina had not grumbled and made their home look as nice as possible. The young couple saved as much money as they could from their wages to buy the furniture and things they needed. They were always so happy and loved each other very much. Their joy was complete when the twins were born. Of course, Tina was not able to work while they were small, but they managed somehow to have enough money for their needs.

The twins were bright children and once they started at school both reached the top of their class very quickly. Tina had great hopes for them that they would go to secondary school and then get good jobs. Much as she loved Len, she knew she wanted better for her two 'Freds', as she had nicknamed her children.

"Tina, why did you catch consumption and die? Why did you leave me?" Len was questioning in his mind. "If only you were still here, how different things would have been!"

During his wife's illness he had become more and more frightened and this had made him angry. He began to drink and sometimes, as much as he loved his wife, he was violent towards her. When he was sober he felt so ashamed of himself and promised never to do such things again. Sadly, his promises didn't last.

After Tina's long illness and eventual death Len just went to pieces. He couldn't cope without his wife. The twins, even though they were devastated and motherless, tried to look after the house and home, but all Len did was drink more and more ale, trying to drown out his thoughts. He felt so guilty that he could not take care of his family properly.

As Len sat and thought on that Sunday afternoon, he felt so ashamed of himself—such a failure. He now owed the landlord of The Cock and Hen a large sum of money. The only way to get out of the mess had been to sell his daughter to the man. He knew it was a terrible thing to do. Winnie didn't deserve such a bleak future. Will didn't deserve the workhouse either, but it was the only way that Len could think his son would be looked after and be placed into some sort of apprenticeship. Horrible though it was, he thought his son might have some sort of future that way.

When Tina had died the thought had occurred to Len that he perhaps could write to his father-in-law and tell him about his daughter's death. However, when the twins had been born, Tina had written to tell her family, but there had been no reply. She felt they had been so angry with her that she would never be forgiven or accepted by them again. Len had too much pride to contact them now.

Thinking about these things made Len feel very, very angry. One of the people with whom he felt very angry was the landlord. He felt he had been tricked somehow and that the man had taken advantage of his weakness.

Suddenly, Len felt his head was going to burst. He had to do something. He had to be a man!

He got up and tried to walk to the bar, but he was very unsteady on his feet. He had drunk too much. The landlord looked at him.

"Why don't you go and get your lovely Winnie now?" he suggested. "Let her come tonight. She can 'elp me with the kiddies right away. Then I'll give you an extra jug of beer!"

Len saw red. Never had he been so angry, but mostly it was with himself. He picked up his empty tankard and threw it with all his might at the landlord and it hit him smack in the eye.

Within minutes there was a huge fight going on and it seemed that everyone in the pub joined in on one side or the other. Len didn't own a knife, but someone did and that person attacked the landlord, wounding him very badly. No one saw who did it and in minutes they heard a police whistle and almost everyone disappeared very quickly. Those who remained were only too eager to tell the policeman that Len had attacked the landlord, so he was arrested, not just for being drunk and disorderly, but for attempted murder.

An ambulance took the landlord to the hospital, for he was in a bad way, and Len was taken to the police cells.

He lay on the stone floor and wished that he had been knifed, not the landlord. To die would be to join his beloved Tina. Then he thought again, maybe he wouldn't join her. He was a bad man, full of hate, anger and bitterness. She had been kind and gentle and loved to go to the church and taught the children about God. No wonder that Winnie had wanted to go today. What about Winnie? What would happen to her now? Would she be sent to the workhouse too? Len really deep down in his heart adored his children. He had let them down so badly!

Chapter Nine

Will walked back to the workhouse after church feeling so much more cheerful. He had seen Winnie and she looked fine and she had passed him a note. He couldn't wait to get back and find somewhere safe to read it! In his excitement he began to take big strides, forgetting for a few minutes that Eric couldn't keep up.

"Fred Collins—keep in line!" shouted the Master, who was behind him. "And you, Eric Lyons, get a move on—keep up with the boys!"

Both boys tried to keep in step and eventually they arrived back at the workhouse. They were glad it was Sunday for there was less work to do and dinner was the best meal of the week.

The boys were given meat on Sundays and although it was rather tough mutton, nevertheless, it tasted very good to them all. After dinner they helped with the clearing away but after that had some free time. Will raced to his dormitory and sat on his bed. He took Winnie's letter out of his pocket and smiled as he saw she had written it in their secret code. How clever of her! If anyone discovered it, the message would be safe!

He didn't need a pencil to decipher it—he knew the code so well in his head.

He started with the vowels.

A =V & V=A; E = W & W = E; I = X & X = I; O = Y & Y = O; U = Z & Z = U.

The rest of the alphabet went like this.

B = F & F = B; G = C & C = G; D =H & H = D; J = P & P = J; K = Q & Q = K; L = R & R = L; M =S & S = M; N = T & T = N.

Soon Will had read the secret message. Can you do it?

He was shocked by what he read. How could his Pa want his sister to do such a thing? Although he could understand why Winnie had run away, he felt so sad that he wouldn't see her on Sunday mornings and had no idea where she would go. Had she gone already? He thought of what the minister had said in the sermon—that God loved and cared for them all and that at any time, anywhere, they could pray to Him.

"Please, God, if that's true, then take care of Winnie. Help me somehow to get out of this place and look after her. Amen."

He felt a little better after praying that prayer, but with a heavy heart he climbed off his bed and went out to the yard where most of the boys were playing games. He saw Eric on his own as usual, but he was playing 'Jacks' with some small stones. Will went to join him and tried to forget his problems by playing with his friend.

Will gradually became used to the workhouse routine. It was certainly harsh, but not everyone was unkind. The boys slowly accepted him and within a few days two brothers were admitted, so he was no longer the new boy or bullied so much. He went out of his way to be kind to the newcomers as well as to Eric. The best part of the day for him was school. He just loved to learn and the schoolmaster even lent him a book to read about ancient Greece. Because he was so good at maths the teacher asked him to help some of the younger boys who were struggling and Will found that he really enjoyed teaching them. Maybe one day, he would be a school teacher too! Will knew that it was an almost impossible dream, but he still loved to think that he might just have a future.

Sometimes, he wondered about his family. He knew his Pa had left school when he was very young and couldn't read or write, but that was very common among the working class, as people like him were called in Victorian times. He didn't know if his father had parents— he had always thought they must be dead for they had never been mentioned. His Mam had told the twins, just before she died, that her family were not from this part of the county, but lived in a very large house, some way to the south and she had run away to marry their Pa. Until now he had never thought about having grandparents, uncles, aunts or cousins.

A week or two after Winnie had run away, Will was summoned to the Master's office.

He was a bit scared as he was taken by Matron through the endless corridors. Had he done something wrong? He had tried so hard to keep all the rules and work hard.

The Matron knocked at the Master's door and they heard him call, "Come in!"

"In you go, boy," said the Matron sharply, almost pushing Will inside.

In the office, alongside the Master was a police officer.

Will drew in his breath quickly. What was wrong? Had Winnie been found?

"Now, Fred," said the Master, "the policeman wants to ask you some questions."

Will turned his head to the officer.

"Yes, sir?" he asked. "How can I help you?"

"'Tis about your father. He went off and left you 'ere and I 'ave to tell you that you won't be seeing him for a long, long time. Locked up and to be deported he is and a good job too. Nasty bit of work, I tell you."

"I don't understand, sir," said Will, quite shocked, if what he was thinking was true. Was his Pa in prison?

"Your father was in a fight and he is to be sent to Australia for ten years' hard labour for assault and attempted murder."

"What, my Pa? He can't be," said Will. "He gets drunk at times, especially since Mam died and can be a bit, well, violent when roused, but he's always sorry and he wouldn't ever try to murder anyone."

"I'm afraid he did and I have come to tell you so. The Landlord has repossessed your house and the goods have been sold to pay off the rent. Your sister has disappeared into thin air. I trust he didn't murder her too!" said the policeman, almost as if it was a joke.

"Of course he wouldn't do that. He's not really a bad man," said Will at once, but secretly terrified that perhaps Pa had found

Winnie after she had run away and done something terrible to her. Pa certainly would be furious she had run away. Oh how he hoped she was safe!

"Well, she's not been admitted here—yet," said the Master. "If she is, you will be told, although you would not be allowed to see her. Now off you go! I'll be keeping a special eye out for you, lad. I'll make sure you don't turn out like your father, you can be sure of that!"

The Master turned to the police officer as Will went to open the door.

"Bad blood there. I will keep a good eye on him. He's too clever for his own good too!"

Leaving the room, Will could see by the look on Matron's face that she had listened at the door and heard it all. She had always treated him as if he were an insect on the floor—would it get even worse now?

Will struggled to get his head around the news. What had his Pa done to get himself deported for so long? At least he wasn't on 'death row' and waiting for hanging. The judge must have been a bit lenient with the punishment. Maybe he wasn't guilty, but poor people could not afford to have a lawyer to represent them.

The doubt had been planted in Will's mind about Winnie's safety. He had heard nothing after that first letter and wondered if she had managed to get away. If not, what had happened to her? They no longer had a house or Mam's nice furniture that she was so proud of. Will felt desperate. What could he do? If only he could escape from the workhouse!

At lunch that day Matron gave an announcement.

"Keep away from Fred," she said. "His father is in prison awaiting deportation to Australia for a very long time! He attempted to murder someone! He's from an evil family! Shun him! Shun evil as the good book says!"

"Come up here, Fred," Matron shouted. Fred left his thin cabbage soup and walked to the front of the dining hall. Matron held a placard which she put over his head and it read, "Keep your distance. I have bad blood. I am evil."

Poor Will. Most of the boys loved to have someone to bully and treat badly. Now his life would be even more difficult!

"Stand here for the rest of the lunch break and you will wear this notice all of this week, including when you walk to church!"

"Yes, Matron," answered Will still trying to be calm and polite, even though he was nearly boiling with rage inside.

It was so unfair! Why should he be punished for his Pa? Why did people hate him so?

Eric was at his side as soon as the boys were dismissed from the meal.

"Don't worry about her. I'm still your friend and everyone will soon forget about it. At least you've got a Pa and knew your Mam and have a sister. I ain't got anyone to call my own!"

When the boys came to the classroom the next morning the teacher was so sad to see the notice hung around Will's neck. He hated the way that the boys were treated just because they were poor. The workhouse was supposed to help poor people and show God's love to them, but all he saw was hate and cruelty. In many ways he hated teaching there, but he felt it was where God wanted him to be, to help the children who couldn't help themselves. If they could be educated then maybe they could get a better life when they were adults.

"Dear God," he prayed silently, "how can I help this lad?"

Chapter Ten

Most of the boys in the workhouse soon forgot about bullying Will. He was a natural sportsman and they all wanted him on their team when it was recreation time and they were playing games. He was good tempered too and willing to help them with reading and maths homework. However, he felt so humiliated by the placard which remained around his neck and was horrified that he had to wear it on Sunday to St. Cuthbert's church. He knew that some of his old school friends, like Madge and her family, would be there and see it. For once he was very glad that Winnie would not be in church. How he wished he would hear from her!

When Sunday arrived, in spite of Will's humiliation and embarrassment, the placard turned out to be a help for him. The minister was very angry when he saw it around his neck and challenged the Master.

"Why is that lad wearing such a terrible label?" he asked, as the boys filed out of the church.

"His father has been found guilty of attempted murder and is in prison waiting for deportation to Australia. We will watch him like a hawk to make sure he doesn't develop a bad character too. We can't be too careful with training these lads, you know," answered the

Master smugly.

"What is the lad's name and how old is he?" enquired the minister, determined that he would do something about the situation.

"He's Fred Collins, well, his full name is Wilfred and he's eleven. His mother is dead, his sister disappeared into thin air. The constable thinks she could have been murdered by her father too. I guess I'll have to train him until he gets apprenticed somewhere. The schoolmaster says he's good with his numbers and letters."

As the boys marched away, the minister was even more determined to see if he could help Will. That afternoon he went to visit the school teacher, for they were good friends. He learnt more of Will's story and they prayed together asking God to show them how they could help the lad.

"He's the most intelligent lad I have ever taught since I went to work in the workhouse," he told Rev. Franklin. "He's always polite, good at sports, loves to learn and also helps the younger boys. It's hard to believe that he has an illiterate father who is now being deported. That lad should have a chance to make something of himself, but the Master of the workhouse and the boys' Matron both despise him and always try to humiliate him. I'm afraid they will apprentice him in a very unsuitable place out of sheer spite."

"We've asked God to help us and now we must look for His answer," said the minister thoughtfully, as he put on his coat ready to go home.

During the next few days Will kept trying to make an escape plan.

The only time that the boys left the workhouse was to go to church on Sunday. Will was always at the end of the crocodile with Eric and directly behind them was the Master, so it would be very hard to run away. If he came up with a plan, then Eric would have to know and it would make things very bad for him if the Master found out and Will didn't want his friend to get into more trouble.

Will felt that the school teacher was also a friend, but he was a 'grown up' and he wasn't sure that he could really trust him with a secret or ask him to help with an escape. If only Winnie was around, she would help him escape. For the millionth time he wondered where she was, if she was safe and if he would ever see her again!

Happy in her new job and feeling fit and strong with all the exercise, Winnie loved her new life, except for two things. One was the constant worry about her true identity being discovered and the other was a longing to be able to get in contact with Will to find out how he was. She did sometimes think about her Pa too, but mostly those thoughts made her very angry.

"Fred, we are coming to Barnsoldwick and we'll stop there for a meal before we do the Foulridge Tunnel," Dan told her. "I hope you've got loads of energy, for it's a very long tunnel, not the longest on this canal, but about a mile. Mabel is so pleased not to have to 'leg it' through. Your legs will ache something terrible after doing it, but I reckon you'll manage. You've proved very useful so far."

Winnie beamed at the praise. She had tried her best. Clodhoppper was now her great friend and she whispered all sort of things into his ear as they walked the towpath day after day.

Mabel fed her so well—it had been a long time since her family had regularly eaten such good food. She liked to help Mabel too, watching her cook and learning new recipes.

Winnie was a bit frightened by the tunnel. As they approached the entrance, she could see it was very dark and it was so long that there was just a speck of light at the end. It smelt very damp and the walls were running with water. Mabel had taken the horse and was walking him the long way round. Legging the tunnel would take quite a long time. She and Dan went on to the roof of the narrow boat and lay on their backs with their legs in the air. Winnie's legs only just touched the top of the tunnel. As a team, she and Dan using their feet as levers, pushed the boat inch by inch into the tunnel. It was a little like running a marathon. To start with they both had some energy and enthusiasm and once they could see more light at the end of the tunnel they had one last burst of energy to complete the task, but while they were in the middle it was very hard going. Dan tried to get Winnie singing, to help her push in time to the music, but she found it almost impossible to get any breath and push at the same time. At one point she thought she wasn't able to do any more, but she so wanted to keep this job, she loved the canal and had grown very fond of Mabel and Dan. They seemed like the grandparents she had never known!

When they finally emerged from the tunnel, Mabel and Dan both had to help Winnie get off the roof and into the cabin.

"He's all done in!" said Mabel, very concerned. "He's not really a very big lad for eleven and not used to the canal the way our children were. Let him sleep a bit, Dan. Let's moor up here for an hour."

"Alright," agreed Dan, "but only for one hour because we must get through the next lock before nightfall."

When Mabel woke Winnie after an hour with a nice cup of tea, she felt a little better. That was, until she tried to stand on her feet! They were shaky and wobbly and ached all over!

"Never mind, Fred, you'll get stronger. The first tunnel is always the worst and Foulbridge is one of the longest on this canal network. You should be so proud of yourself; you didn't give up! Dan is very pleased with you!" Mabel said.

Winnie felt relieved by that. She didn't want Dan to look for an older, stronger lad to work with him.

"On we go!" said Mabel, "We need to work the next lock before we moor up. You alright to lead Clodhopper?"

Winnie said she would try and was glad to feel the horse's great strength near her. Somehow, it gave her the courage to go on. She really felt exhausted.

They reached the lock and Mabel took Clodhopper to have a drink in the large stone trough which was always filled with water for the horses. Dan stayed on 'Bright Water', ready to steer her into the lock and Winnie had jumped off and was helping to open the large wooden gate. She was never quite sure what happened next, but suddenly she had slipped and her legs gave way underneath her completely. She fell into the lock and although she could swim, her head hit the lock wall as she fell and the cold, dark water swirled around her. It felt as if she was being swallowed up by some dirty, muddy monster and everything went black.

It took Dan a few moments to realise what had happened, then to steer the boat into the lock, all the time calling to the lock keeper for help! He grabbed his long boat hook, hoping to hold it as a life line for Winnie. Mabel was crying and praying and feeling utterly helpless as she watched in horror.

"I see him!" shouted Dan. "But he's not swimming. I'll get him … pray I do," and he managed to fasten the boat hook onto Winnie's trousers and pull her up. Things didn't look good. Her lips were blue and she wasn't breathing. The lock keeper had jumped on board and together the men began to lift Winnie and expel the water from her lungs. Then they began to breathe into her lungs and suddenly she spluttered, spitting out some mud and weed.

"Come on Fred, breathe for us," prayed Dan, continuing to give artificial respiration to Winnie. Gradually, she began to breathe properly and her lips went pink again. Everyone sighed with relief!

"Thank God!" said the lock keeper.

"Yes, thank God indeed," answered Dan and Mabel, as Mabel wrapped a shivering Winnie in a blanket.

"What a good job that Dan had learnt some first aid too. Neither of us can swim, so we couldn't jump in and help!"

"Right," said the lock keeper. "Mabel, run over to our cottage and tell the missus to heat some water for a bath. We must warm this lad up or he'll get pneumonia. Meanwhile, we must get this lock sorted and get you out the other side, so that you can moor up properly."

Once they were moored, Dan carried the still shivering child over to the lock keeper's house which was very near. A tin bath had been filled with warm water and despite the feeble protests of Winnie, Mabel undressed her and put her into the bath. Her whole body was muddy and smelly and her hair matted.

Winnie's secret was out! Mabel gently washed her, as if she were her own daughter and then wrapped her in a towel which the lock keeper's wife had provided. She rubbed her down, trying to improve the circulation and keep Winnie from shivering and then she covered her in a clean, dry blanket.

Winnie began to cry softly. Now Mabel knew she was a girl, would she and Dan turn her out? What would happen to her now?

Chapter Eleven

"You need some dry clothes, dear," Mabel said to Winnie, "Have you got any?"

"In the bundle I brought with me, not the bundle wrapped in my shawl, but the other one," whispered Winnie hoarsely, still trying to cough up the canal water she had swallowed.

In a few minutes Mabel returned with the bundle. As she opened it, Winnie's long hair fell out, tied in two plaits, just as it was when she had cut it off. Then Mabel took out the clothes and started to dress Winnie in them.

"I think as soon as you are better you must tell Dan and I who you really are. Then we will think about what to do," Mabel told her. "I had my suspicions all along that you were a girl, but I didn't say anything to him." Mabel began to chuckle. "He was proper taken in by you. What a shock he will have when I tell him you're not a lad at all! What are we going to call you now?"

"My real name is Winifred. Most people call me Winnie, but my mam always called my twin brother Wilfred and I her 'Two Freds'," replied Winnie, trying very hard not to cry. It had been a terrible day and she wondered if the couple would now tell her to leave.

Mabel saw her tears and bent down and kissed her forehead.

"Now my lass, don't take on so," she comforted Winnie. "We'll work something out. You are already like one of the family to us and all we want is for you to get well quickly. Mrs Lock Keeper is making you a bowl of hot bread and milk. They keep their own cow here, so the milk is extra special! I'm going over to 'Bright Water' now to make up the couch for you and get the fire stoked up, then Dan can carry you home!"

Winnie tried to eat the bread and milk which had been sweetened with a little sugar as a very special treat. Everyone was being so kind and she knew she didn't deserve such treatment. By the time that Dan came to collect her, she was fast asleep and he carried her gently to the narrow boat.

The next day Winnie woke up feeling much better. Her head was still sore where she had banged it against the lock wall and her legs still ached a lot, but she wanted to be up and working as soon as possible. She didn't want to lose her job! She knew that Dan and Mabel could not afford to lose a day's work because they would be penalised if they didn't get their cargo to its destination on time. She was also dreading the 'talk' which she knew she must have with her employers! She looked for her boy's clothes, but they were nowhere to be seen, so she dressed in her old dress and petticoats and it felt so nice not to have the rough trousers rubbing against her legs!

"Well now, look at you, Fred, up and dressed ready for your breakfast," said Dan with a beaming smile. "I'm so glad. I have been worrying all night that my helper might be too sick to work today.

I shouldn't have worked you so hard legging the tunnel. I'm really sorry!"

"Can I still work for you then?" Winnie asked. "Even though I am a girl?"

"You've proved yourself, haven't you?" he replied. "You have managed everything I asked you to do, so I have no reason to sack you!"

Winnie was so relieved she gave Dan a big hug and then went to fetch the water and feed for Clodhopper. The day went smoothly and they made good progress. Winnie still didn't feel very strong, but she was so happy to be able to keep her job that she tried to forget her headache and wobbly legs.

That evening, before they read from her little Bible and prayed together, Winnie knew she had some explaining to do. She felt very sorry that she had deceived Dan and Mabel and asked them to forgive her. Then she told them her story, all about her Mam, Pa and Will. She told them why she had run away and Mabel put her arm around her and said she understood and that it was probably for the best.

"Maybe I should drop my hair into the canal tomorrow," Winnie said.

"Oh no! Don't do that!" exclaimed Mabel. "In Liverpool you can sell it. You can get a good price for it, because it can be made into a wig. I'll take you to a barber who will buy it!"

"What about my clothes?" asked Winnie. "If I am to still leg in the tunnels, then I can't really do that in my dress and petticoats!"

"I'll wash your brother's clothes and they will come in handy for jobs like that. As for other clothes, well, I'll look in my trunk and I'm sure we can do a few alterations and make you some more. I always wanted a daughter to help me, although I love my three big sons to bits!" Mabel answered.

"Now I would like you to read to us, if you don't mind," asked Dan. "Can you read from St. John's gospel, the part about the Good Shepherd?"

Winnie read aloud chapter ten. It made the tears come again.

"I ran away like that sheep which got lost, didn't I?" she said to the couple. "I really need to ask Jesus to forgive me and thank Him that he didn't let me die yesterday. I thought I was going to drown."

The three of them all were so grateful to the Lord that Winnie was safe and well and thanked Him so much for her rescue.

"Thank you too, dear Father, for giving us Winnie to share our home. Help us to be like grandparents to her for as long as she needs us," prayed Mabel. This almost made Winnie cry again!

"And look after Will in the workhouse and help me to get a letter to him," prayed Winnie. "And help me to forgive my Pa. I know I ought to but I just feel angry and hateful towards him."

In a prison cell in Lancashire, Len Collins was also feeling angry. He was angry with everything and everyone, but most of all with himself. He hated himself for the way he had treated his wife when she had become ill and also for the way he had treated his children.

How could he have behaved so badly! Instead of working hard to support them, all he had done was turned to drink to 'drown his sorrows' as the saying goes and had even become violent through the last years. It was like a slippery slope and once he had started down the path, he couldn't seem to stop his bad habits. Now look where he had ended up! He was in prison waiting to be deported to Australia for a crime he hadn't committed. Nobody would believe he was innocent and he really wasn't surprised.

Since he had been locked up, Len had had plenty of time to think and no beer to dull those thoughts. He was scared of going to another continent and having to serve ten years of hard labour. Would he survive the sea journey and would he ever see his children again? They would be adults—twenty-one years old by the time he was freed! Len had never even seen the sea and had little idea how long it would take to reach Australia. He wasn't able to read or write. He didn't even know if people spoke English in the colony. Deep down Len was very, very scared. He wished his wife was still alive; she would have prayed for him. Of course, if she had been alive, then everything would have been so different! He knew he should be thankful he had not been hung on the gallows, but he dreaded the future.

From the cold, dark prison he cried out to the God whom his wife had loved so much.

"O God, if you really exist, please have mercy on me and the twins!"

Chapter Twelve

"Fred Collins," called Matron one morning at breakfast, "you are to report at once to the Master."

"Now what?" thought Will as he left the room and found the porter ready to escort him along the many corridors of the workhouse. It wasn't that he didn't know the way, but boys were never allowed to leave their wing on their own, in case they might try to escape! That was just what Will wanted to do and had been thinking up ways of how he might manage it.

He knocked on the door of the Master's office.

"Enter," he was told.

"I have a report here from the school teacher. He says you are working hard and very good at your lessons and you help the smaller boys as well. Since you are so good with your letters and numbers I think we should send you out to earn your keep. Although you are still a bit young I am looking to apprentice you somewhere, where you can use your learning. Maybe you can learn to be a clerk or a book keeper."

"Yes, sir," replied Will, not really knowing what he was supposed to say. He knew he would have no choice, but maybe it would be a way out of the workhouse and then he could find Winnie and look after her.

"You may go … I almost forgot. A letter arrived for you. It's a load of rubbish. I almost burnt it, but since you are here, you might as well have it."

"Thank you, sir," Will said quietly, taking an envelope which had been torn open. He was angry that his private letter had been opened but expected no better treatment.

It was time for school, so Will put the letter in his pocket, longing for the time when he could read it. He was sure it was from Winnie and he so wanted to know where she was and what she was doing.

In the classroom Will explained to the teacher that he was to be apprenticed as soon as the Master could find a place for him. This worried his teacher because once the papers were signed then Will would not be able to leave the job for five or seven years, however good or bad the apprenticeship proved to be. Now that his Pa was in prison and being deported, the workhouse Master would act as legal guardian and he didn't have the best interest of Will at heart. Indeed, he seemed to have taken a real dislike to the lad. The teacher decided he would have to try and do something about the situation but needed to act really quick. Once the Master had made up his mind to apprentice Will, then he would do so as soon as possible. The school teacher was so pleased it was coming to the weekend. It gave him Sunday to talk to the minister at St. Cuthbert's and see if between them they could help in any way. He knew how much the Rev. Franklin cared about all the inmates of the workhouse and they met to pray for them from time to time.

The morning seemed to drag by for Will. He tried to concentrate and work hard, but all the time he was thinking about the letter in his pocket from his sister. He had to wait until school was finished and dinner time was over. Matron was so horrid that if she saw the letter she probably would take it from him and tear it up!

As soon as he could, Will went out to the privy where he knew he would not be disturbed. He took out the letter and read:

HWVL EXRR,
X VS YT V TVLLYE FYVN GVRRWH FLXCDN EVNWL VTH
EYLQXTC DVLH SVQXTC SO EVO NY RXAWLJYYR.
DYJW OYZ VLW VRLXCDN. X SXMM OYZ,
EXND RYAW, EXTTXN.

Slowly, he deciphered the code and so was able to understand the message. Once again he was so very glad that they had their own secret code. When they had made it up just for fun, they had no idea that one day it would be so useful!

Will felt so much better once he had news from Winnie. However, he realised that he might now have another problem. Soon he'd be sent to be an apprentice and the usual custom was that an apprentice would live at his place of work and so any letters sent to the workhouse would not reach him. The Master had almost withheld this letter. As Winnie was on a boat, she didn't have an address either, so he could not reply. He was afraid they would lose touch with each other.

Carefully, folding the letter and putting it back in his pocket, Will said a quick prayer as he left the privy.

"Dear God, I know I don't talk to you very well and I don't think about you very often, but I want to ask you to help me. Mam always said you would help us and Rev. Franklin told us that 'at any time, anywhere, we can pray to You.' Please help Winnie and me to keep in touch. Please keep her safe. Please let me have a good apprenticeship and please take care of Eric when I'm gone. I know it's a lot to ask and I don't deserve it, but please hear my prayer, amen."

Will returned to the boy's part of the workhouse and because it was Saturday afternoon he had several chores to do. The boys all had to help clean the building as well as prepare vegetables and do their own laundry. It was very hard work, especially for the smaller boys and those like Eric who were not so strong. It was supposed to be good training for life, but in reality, it was just slave labour!

That afternoon because Will was so happy about his letter and somehow his prayer had made him less worried about his problems, he found himself singing as he worked.

"One man went to mow, went to mow a meadow," he sang—a song he had learnt at his former school. Soon he had other boys joining in and the cleaning time passed quickly. Matron scowled as she heard the singing, but she didn't stop them. The work was getting done and that was all she cared about.

"We ought to sing more often," commented Eric. "That was the best Saturday afternoon for ages. Can you teach us some more songs?"

"Guess I could," Will replied, "but I won't be here much longer because the Master wants to send me out as an apprentice very soon."

"I knew it was too good to be true," said Eric with a very glum face. "You are my best friend and now you are going away!"

"I'll always be your friend and if they'll let me, I'll come to visit you on Saturdays and if I'm still able to go to church, I'll see you there. I promise I'll do my best to see you, Eric."

Eric nodded, but Will could see that he wasn't convinced.

The school teacher lived alone. He was quite an elderly man, whose wife had died in childbirth with their first baby, many years ago. The baby had been a girl and had died at birth, so he had no family. That is why he devoted himself to caring for the boys in the workhouse. He hated the way they were treated. They were given no rights, never treated with dignity or kindness. Mostly, they were good lads; they had just never had a chance in life. He longed to make a difference and from time to time he had been able to help in some small way. Now he so wanted to help Will.

That Saturday afternoon he called on the minister of St. Cuthbert's church.

"You know how I told you about the new lad Fred Collins and that I was concerned about his future," the teacher reminded the minister, "and how we have been praying about how we might help him?"

"Yes, I do," replied the minister, "I've thought and prayed a lot about his situation."

"Well, now it's become critical," the teacher continued and went on to explain about the plans for him to be apprenticed.

"I guess it might happen even next week and that lad could be sent somewhere quite unsuitable. He's such a bright, polite lad. I really want to help him. He could be such a good teacher, given the chance," the teacher explained.

"I did have a thought in my prayer time," the minister replied, "but I haven't done anything about it. My sister runs a 'Dame's School' in Skipton. I thought I would ask her if she would like an apprentice teacher. I just haven't got around to it. Have you got time to come with me if I get out the pony and trap and go there?"

"Certainly. If she felt she could help, it would be just grand!" answered the teacher.

A few minutes later the two men, plus the minister's dog and a basket of goodies which the minister's wife had quickly packed into a basket for her sister-in-law, set off to Skipton. It was a nice afternoon to drive through the countryside and the men enjoyed seeing the newborn lambs skipping in the fields. They arrived at the little market town just as the market stallholders were packing up their wares. Near the castle they turned into a side road and soon were by a Georgian house which stood back from the road. They drove through the wrought iron gates and up the path to the front door. A young man came and untethered the horse, leading him around the back to give him a drink.

"Thank you, Jack," said the minister, as he rang the large bell by the side of the door.

A young girl appeared, wearing a maid's dress, apron and mop cap.

"Good afternoon, Polly," the minister greeted the maid. "Mr Johns and I have come to see my sister."

"Come in, sirs," she said and led the two men into the front parlour, taking their coats and hats. The minister handed her the basket and his dog followed her into the kitchen.

"Hugh," said his sister, "what an unexpected surprise!"

"Maud, meet Mr Johns, a friend of mine. Paul, this is my sister, Miss Franklin," said Rev. Franklin, introducing them.

Soon the reason for their visit was explained, as they drank tea and ate little fairy cakes together.

"I meant to come a few days ago and talk about this lad, but now the situation is urgent," her brother told her.

"What you tell me about Fred sounds very promising. I was praying about help for the school. I now have forty pupils and really that is too many. I had thought about hiring a girl. Most of the older pupils are girls but we do have quite a lot of small boys not yet old enough to be sent away to boarding school.

"I'm not sure that I would want to make Fred an apprentice as such, with indentures and all the legal papers, but if he was willing to come on a trial basis, say for a month, then we could see how things work out for the future."

"So you are willing to help Fred?" said Mr Johns in excitement. "That is so wonderful! When could he start?"

"Well, I need to talk to Jack, my 'outside' lad. He lives above the stable and would have to share his room with Fred for now. Hugh, my dear," Maud turned to her brother, "you will have to help me make some sort of contract about food and wages and that sort of thing. Can you stay and do that now? If so, then I could drive over to you on Monday morning and you can take me to meet Fred. It won't work if we don't like each other!

"I don't want to force any child to work for me as a slave. There's too much of that going on in our land! We get so much talk in Parliament about abolition of slavery and right though that is, we also need to think about the poor children of our land who are pretty well sold into slavery!"

"Absolutely, my dear," Rev. Franklin beamed at his sister, agreeing wholeheartedly. "Let's sort out these working arrangements now and then we'll be off. I have services to take tomorrow!"

Somehow, when the two men went to talk to Jack about a roommate, they made it sound so attractive to him that he eagerly agreed to Will coming and sharing his room. He thought he would like to have a friend to talk with!

The minister and the teacher drove off in high spirits, thanking God for answering their prayers for Fred. All they had to do now was to persuade the Master of the workhouse, but since he was a bit in awe of the minister, who was also a board member of the workhouse, they didn't anticipate too much trouble.

Chapter Thirteen

Most of the boys in the workhouse looked forward to Sunday, even if they didn't understand what church was about. It was wonderful to get outside the building that was almost a prison for them. Several new boys had joined the group since Will had been admitted, but he still liked to walk at the back of the line, to help Eric along. Usually, the Matron was at the front of the boys' crocodile and the Master at the rear.

They were reaching the church when the teacher came up to the Master and asked for a word, so he stepped aside, leaving Eric and Will to go into the porch. The porch was a bit gloomy and nobody except Eric noticed a large man enter and grab hold of Will's arm, put his hand over his mouth and drag him away. He was gone in a flash. Eric screamed, but by the time the Master and teacher had taken notice, other people were surrounding Eric, supposing him to be hurt, and in the confusion the kidnapper got clean away with his victim.

Finally, the teacher was able to calm Eric but was very distressed to hear what had happened and went running in every direction to try and find Will. The Master went purple in the face. He was sure that it was some sort of plot and Will had tried to escape. He thought it must be why he had received the coded letter.

"How stupid I was. It must have been in code! An escape plan! I said that boy had bad blood. I was right! He won't get away with this!" he muttered to himself, almost exploding in anger.

"What exactly did you see?" the Master asked Eric. Eric shook as he saw how angry the Master was. He stuttered as he tried to tell what happened. The teacher came back to the church without success. There was no trace of Will.

"We had better call the police," said the teacher. "This is kidnapping!"

"Why on earth would anyone want to kidnap a guttersnipe like that boy!" replied the Master, "I tell you, he has devised some plan to escape!"

"I don't think so, but in either case, the police must be called at once. You lose that boy and your job could be on the line!" said the teacher with unusual authority. "I'm going to tell Rev. Franklin what has happened so that the congregation can pray. Also, someone might have seen something or someone suspicious and be able to help find Fred."

A few minutes later Mr Johns came out of the church and took Eric by the hand. He spoke to the Master.

"You had better stay with the rest of the boys. I will take Eric and go to the police station and report the kidnapping. I will then bring him back to the workhouse when he has given his evidence."

"Don't be afraid," he said to Eric. "The police are here to help us and all you have to do is try to remember all you saw. It might help us to find Fred. I'm sure he didn't have an escape plan. He didn't say anything odd to you, did he? I know he is your friend."

"No, sir," answered Eric. "He did talk about having to be an apprentice and hoping it would be a good job and that he would come and visit me on Saturdays if he could or see me at church on Sundays if he was still allowed to do that."

The police station was quite a scary place for Eric, but Mr Johns was very kind and would not let the policeman get impatient with him. Although it had happened so quickly in the gloom of the porch, as Eric thought about the incident he was able to tell the policeman that the man was tall and well built, with a big belly and had a red scar on his right cheek going right down to his neck. It stood out, like it was a new scar. Even though the man had a red spotted neckerchief around his neck, it didn't cover it up.

"That's really helpful, son," said the policeman kindly. "You have been very observant! It should help us find this man."

They told the police all they knew about Fred, where he had lived, his twin sister, what had happened to his father and mother.

"His name is Wilfred and all his family called him Will," related Eric. "Only in the workhouse is he called Fred and that upset him because it was his mother's nickname for both him and his sister, Winifred. She called them her 'Two Freds'. Please, please find him quickly before anything horrible happens to him," pleaded Eric, tears in his eyes.

Mr Johns led Eric back to the workhouse after the interview and promised to keep him updated with any news. Then he made his way to the vicarage to talk over the situation with the minister and to pray with him for Will's safety. He was very worried about the lad.

It had all happened so quickly that Will was bewildered. He was grabbed by the arm and couldn't scream for help because a huge hand was over his mouth. Within seconds he was being taken down an alley running between two terraces of back to back houses. After a while he began to recognise the area. It was near his home in Coronation Street. What was going on? Then his captor took his hand off his mouth and revealed who he was. It was none other than the landlord of The Cock and Hen tavern.

"Why have you taken me?" asked Will, trying not to show how scared he was.

"It's because of your Pa. Look what he did to me!" answered the landlord, pointing to the ugly scar on his face and neck. "He broke his agreement too. Your sister was to have come and worked for me both at home and in the tavern. Then she disappeared into thin air—so I figured that you would be better than nothing!"

Will was taken into The Cock and Hen and down to the cellars.

"We will keep you here for a while. Don't want the police finding you. Neither do I want you escaping—so I'm tying you up. No one will hear you if you scream—these cellars are very deep, to keep the ale cool. They'll keep you cool too, and the rats will keep you company!"

Having tied Will's hands and feet, the landlord pushed him to the ground and disappeared.

It took Will a while to understand what it was all about. He pieced two and two together and then understood more why Winnie had run away. She must have heard where their Pa was sending her to work and that the landlord had plans to eventually marry her. He was glad she had run away! It would have been a terrible place for her to have lived, almost like a slave. Will almost felt glad that the landlord had been injured, though somehow he still couldn't believe his Pa had done that. Yes, he used his fists when he was full of drink, but he had never carried a knife or any other weapon.

It was dark in the cellar and it took Will a little while for his eyes to adjust so that he could see the barrels stored there. He could hear scampering from time to time and guessed it was from the rats. He wasn't very keen on those, but once again, he was glad it wasn't Winnie in the cellar as she was terrified of rodents.

Nothing seemed to happen for ages and Will had a lot of time to think. Everything had gone wrong since his Mam had become sick. He tried to think back to the good times when they had been a happy family, but it seemed a very long time ago. He remembered how his Mam had read Bible stories to him and Winnie and prayed with them before they went to bed. She had always told them that the Lord God loved them and had good plans for their lives. It didn't seem that it could be true. His life had become worse and worse but maybe he would try to pray. If God was real then perhaps he would listen. Will wondered if a prayer from a child mattered. Surely, God must be very busy will all the millions of people in the world and all the important people asking him for things. He probably was busy listening to someone like Queen Victoria and not at all bothered about a lad tied up in a dark cellar!

Then Will realised that he had nothing to lose. There was absolutely no one to help him except God.

Lying down with wrists and ankles sore from being tied up, Will screwed his eyes up tightly and whispered,

"Dear God, if I can pray to you any time, anywhere, like the minister told us, please listen to me. I'm in an awful jam here. This is even worse than the workhouse. I don't like that man the landlord and I'm scared. Please rescue me. And please, if it's not too much to ask, take great care of Winnie and one day let us be together again. Amen."

After his prayer Will fell asleep. He slept until he was woken by the noise of someone coming down the stone stairs. He had no idea what the time was because it was so dark and the only light came from a grating at the end of the cellar.

Then he saw a small figure carrying a candle.

"I've brought you some bread and cheese, Will, and a mug of water. I'll look after you, but don't tell Pa or he'll kill me!" said a lad who was about the same age as Will. Will looked at him and recognised the son of the landlord, Percy. They had been in the same class at school when Percy had been allowed to go. Most of the time he had to help his Pa at home.

"Percy! How glad I am to see you!" said Will. "And I'm very hungry. There's not much food in the workhouse. Can you untie my wrists so that I can eat?"

Percy put the food and water on the top of a barrel and quickly undid the knots. Will rubbed his wrist and then grabbed the food.

"I'll stay and chase the rats away! As soon as they smell food they will be all over you!" Percy told him.

"Where is your Pa now?" asked Will.

"It's Sunday, so he's gone out poaching with some mates. He won't be back for a while—not until its dark, so you'll be safe. I'd love to help you escape, but I'm too afraid to do that. When he's angry, Pa can really beat the living daylights out of me. If we're careful I can make sure you get food and I'll tie you up loosely. He won't let you out of here until the hue and cry has died down," Percy told him.

"He's still really angry about being attacked and then going to the hospital. He had a big bill to pay for that," Percy explained, "and he seems to think it was all your Pa's fault."

"Was it?" asked Will sadly. "I know he gets into fights, but I've never known him to carry a weapon. You know he's in prison and going to Australia on the next convict ship?"

"So I heard," Percy answered. "It wasn't him, though. He didn't try to kill Pa. Your Pa started the fight and then everyone joined in. It was such a rumpus that we heard it upstairs and I came down and crept into the bar. It was another man who had the knife. When Pa was hurt I scuttled upstairs as quickly as I could in case the man saw me and turned on me. If I got hurt too, then who would look after all the young 'uns? They'd all be in the workhouse before you could blink! I'm sorry your dad was convicted. I was so glad to hear they didn't string him up on the gallows.

"Sorry I can't stay any longer. The little 'uns upstairs will wonder where I am and I don't want them telling tales to Pa. I'll leave you the candle and come back as soon as I can. I'll do my best for you, Will," said Percy, taking the cup and plate and retying Will's wrists, but much less tightly and also loosening the string around his ankles. "Is there anyone I can tell that you are here. Maybe tomorrow when the bar is open I can slip out or send our Lucy."

Will thought for a few moments. Then he had an idea.

"The only person who has been kind to me in the workhouse is the schoolmaster, Mr Johns. I know he is a friend of the minister, Rev. Franklin at St. Cuthbert's church, where your Pa grabbed me. If you could get hold of a pencil and bit of paper, I could write him a note. We'd have to get it to the church somehow, but that might be safer for you than the workhouse," suggested Will.

"I'll do my best," promised Percy, "but please don't tell Pa that I've fed you. He probably won't notice the candle, but if he asks, you can say that I brought it down but was so surprised to see you that I left it when I ran back upstairs. Let's hope he doesn't notice!"

Percy disappeared and Will thought he would ask God to stop the landlord noticing the candle so that his friend wouldn't get into trouble. He closed his eyes once again.

"Dear God, you must be real and must have listened to my prayer. Thank you. Thank you so much for sending Percy with food and a light and please protect him from his Pa's anger and make his Pa not notice this candle. Oh, and one thing more, please can you make this candle last much longer than usual because I hate it here in the dark and with the rats. Amen."

Will thought about his Mam and was glad she had told him how he needed to pray. There was plenty of time to think in that dark cellar. He thought about his life and the times when he had told lies, even to his Mam. Even though he loved his sister, there had been times when he had been mean to her. He wished he could say sorry to both of them, but he knew that he needed to say sorry to God. He knew he had done lots of bad things in his life and remembered how his Mam had told them that Jesus had allowed himself to be captured and falsely condemned to death and had died. He didn't understand very well, but he knew that in some way Jesus had taken the punishment which he deserved for all the wrong things in his life. There in the dark cellar, Will felt so sorry for the things he had done wrong. He knew Jesus had died for him because he loved him. There, tied up like a parcel and imprisoned in a cellar, he asked Jesus to forgive him and to come into his life, just as his Mam had explained to him. The candle seemed to fill the whole cellar with light and Will no longer felt afraid. In fact, he felt as if he was being hugged by someone who loved him very much. The feeling was so wonderful that Will hoped it would never go away!

Chapter Fourteen

W ill found he was listening, all the time, for the sound of heavy footsteps, which might mean the landlord had come home and was coming to the cellar. In fact, he heard rather quiet, hesitant footsteps and was really surprised when the door was opened by a little girl, younger than Percy.

She was carrying a piece of paper and a stub of a pencil and holding another candle in her other hand.

"I'm Lucy," she said. "Percy told me about you. It's alright, he has made me promise to keep it a secret. He says if you write the minister a note right now, he will let me run to the parsonage straight away. I should be back home before Pa, but if I'm not, Pa probably wouldn't even notice—there's so many of us and he'll think I'm out in the privy!"

"You'll have to untie my hands, Lucy. Can you manage that?" asked Will, giving her a huge smile. If he had been able, he would have given her a hug—he was so happy to hear what she had said!

He wrote the note very quickly, asking for the help of the school teacher and saying where he was. Once Lucy had tied his wrists again, he said to her,

"Lucy, thanks ever so much. Don't let any other grown-up see this note, except the minister. If someone else comes along, you'll have to eat it like a spy would! Run quickly and come back safely!"

Lucy giggled and then in a flash she was gone. Afterwards Will felt so much better. He was sure he would soon be rescued, but he also knew that Jesus was with him.

Lucy carefully put the note in her pocket, which was tied around her waist. Then she threw her shawl around her shoulders and ran quickly towards St. Cuthbert's church, which was in the centre of the town. Next door to the church was the parsonage—a large brick built house. She opened the garden gate and ran up the path to the front door. She was a bit scared as she had never been to such a large house before. She heard a dog bark as she rang the bell and that made her even more scared.

The door was opened by a large lady who was wearing an apron and a cap, so she guessed she must be a servant of some kind.

"What is it, child?" she asked. "I hope you've not come here begging. Too many beggars these days!"

"Please, ma'am," answered Lucy. "I'm not a beggar. I have an important message for the minister."

"Well, give it to me then," the woman answered. "I'll take it to him."

"No ma'am, I can't do that," answered Lucy. "I was told to give it to no one except the Rev. Franklin himself."

"He's busy with someone else, child. If you won't give it to me, then come another day!"

"But I can't, ma'am," and Lucy began to cry, for she was only a little girl and really didn't know what to do.

"What's the problem, Martha?" Lucy heard a man say, just as the door was being shut in her face.

As soon as the minister heard the story, he opened the door wide and called Lucy back.

"You have brought a message for me, dear?" he enquired kindly, smiling at the small child who, although she was wearing an old shawl and bonnet, was without shoes. He sighed to himself. How much he hated the poverty which so many people around him had to endure!

Lucy smiled back and reached into her pocket to find the note and proudly handed the message to him.

"It's from Will," she said.

"I don't think I know a lad called Will," said the minister as he unfolded the paper.

"Come in, dear, come in," he said as he read it. "Inside is my dear friend Mr Johns, the schoolmaster from the workhouse. He must read this!"

Lucy was a bit bewildered. The minister didn't know Will, but he seemed very happy to read the note, not sad that Will was a prisoner in their cellar!

Lucy was taken to the kitchen and Martha gave her milk and cake, while the minister went back into his study to share the very good news with his friend.

"We were just praying and here is an answer—it was already on the way!" he said as he handed over the note to the school teacher to read.

"Wonderful! Thank you, Father God!" exclaimed the teacher. "We know where Fred is—let's get the police at once!"

After her drink and cake, Lucy was told to run home and if possible to tell Will that help would soon be on its way.

"I will. Pa hasn't yet come home. Please don't tell him that Percy and I have helped Will. He'll be so angry he'll beat us," begged Lucy.

"Your secret is safe with us. Run home quickly, dear, and thank you for what you have done," said Rev. Franklin.

The instant Lucy had gone, Martha the cook was sent to find the minister's wife.

"Can you get the spare room ready, my dear?" he asked. "We may have a young guest tonight. I'll explain when I get back."

The two men were soon dressed in their capes and hats and on their way to the police station to explain about the help they needed to rescue young Will.

Lucy ran all the way home. She had never had such an adventure in all her life and was longing to tell Percy about the big house, the cook and the food! When she arrived she heard shouting. Oh dear, her Pa was back! She crept in the back door and took off her bonnet and shawl. Then she crept outside again and visited the privy because she knew she would have to tell the truth if her Pa asked where she had been.

He did! "Where have you been, Lucy?" he demanded.

"In the privy, Pa," she replied, glad she could tell the truth.

Her Pa grunted. "Did you want me for something, Pa?" she asked sweetly.

"Get the little 'uns some bread and milk and get them off to bed early tonight. I've got things to do."

"Yes Pa," she answered and went to the scullery to do as she was told, wondering where Percy was as she hadn't seen him. Then she heard him singing the song he had learnt at school, "One man went to mow, went to mow a meadow!" at the top of his voice.

He was in the shed and skinning rabbits, which Pa must have caught in the traps. She knew it was illegal, but the meat was lovely in a stew. Tomorrow they would have a good dinner! She was always a bit scared when her Pa went poaching because if he were caught he could be hung or deported to the colonies. Not that Lucy knew where they were, only that they were far, far away. She wasn't really sure what the 'colonies' were—something to do with Queen Victoria. She only knew that if something happened to her Pa, there was no Mam any more to care for them and they would probably be sent to the workhouse!

Soon Lucy heard her Pa going down to the cellar. She shivered when she thought of Will tied up with all those rats running around.

Down in the cellar the candle had just burnt itself out and Will was feeling cross about that when he heard the dreaded footsteps of the landlord. Then he suddenly thought, "Thank goodness the candle is out!" and he tried to sit up a little more.

The landlord stormed in.

"I've changed my plans!" he told Will. "Just in case the police get wind of where you are, I'm taking you somewhere else to lie low for a few days. They won't bother to look for a workhouse child for very long."

When Will's feet were untied, he rubbed his ankles because they were cold and tingly. His hands were still tied and the Landlord put a gag over his mouth, a large cape around him and a flat cap on his head which was so big it almost covered his face. Then he bundled Will over his shoulder and carried him up the cellar stairs and through the bar.

Will's heart was pounding. He was so disappointed because he was sure he would have been rescued soon—now nobody would know where he had been taken!

Outside the door of the saloon bar on the road was a horse and cart, and the landlord was just dumping Will into the cart when three policeman came rushing up blowing whistles, quickly followed by a pony and trap containing two distinguished-looking gentlemen.

"Stop in the name of the law!" shouted one policeman, while another caught hold of the horse and the third jumped into the cart to stop the landlord driving it away. Soon people were appearing from all the houses round about to see what all the commotion was, and Percy and Lucy rushed out of the house as well.

When the Landlord realised he was cornered, he gave his hands to be handcuffed while the two gentlemen took Will from the cart, untying the gag and the cords from his wrists.

"Are you alright, Fred?" asked the school teacher. He was so relieved to have found the boy.

"Yes, thank you, sir. I am now."

Once the large cape and cap had been taken off, he was able to see Percy and Lucy at the door. He ran over to them and whispered a thank you for their help.

Soon Will was being driven to the parsonage in the pony and trap while the landlord was taken away in handcuffs to the police cells, charged with kidnapping.

A kind neighbour went over to The Cock and Hen and said she would look after the family until further arrangements could be made. Will prayed they would not end up in the workhouse! He wished that he didn't have to go back there but guessed that was where Mr Johns and Rev. Franklin were taking him.

Indeed, they did drive him to the workhouse, but only to inform the Master that he had been found and rescued from a very dangerous situation.

"I will discuss it with the board and from now on I will take charge of this young man, including his future, for you have failed miserably in your duty to keep him safe," said the minister in a very stern voice. The Master gave Will a poisonous look and then looked fearfully at the Rev. Franklin and mumbled some sort of apology.

"My wife is preparing a room for you, Fred. Would you rather we called you Will? You will stay with us for now. We are hoping that you would like to become a student teacher in my sister's school at Skipton, but we have plenty of time to talk about that later. I think you have had enough excitement for one day!" said Rev. Franklin.

"Yes, sir, I really have. Thank you sir, so very much for not sending me back to the workhouse. Yes, please, I would rather be called Will. You see, only my mam ever called me Fred and so that was a special name."

"Well, Will, welcome to your new home!" said the minister as they drove to the stable at the back of the house.

Chapter Fifteen

It was such a relief for Winnie to be able to behave as a girl once again. Mabel found her some clothes such as all the women and girls on the barges wore; a thick woollen skirt and a warm blouse, with a shawl and bonnet to wear outside. Dan and Mabel soon got used to calling her Winnie and life went on much as before except that Dan didn't expect her to do all the heavy work and when they arrived at a town where there were public baths she was able to go with Mabel and really enjoyed getting properly clean! Of course it was most unusual for a girl to have short hair, but usually it was covered by her bonnet and she knew it would soon grow again.

Travelling through the countryside was such fun! Although Winnie did miss school, she was learning so many new things. Mabel taught her the names of the birds which they saw and the ducks which also lived on the canal. To see a kingfisher dart from a tree into the canal to catch a fish in the early morning was the most amazing sight! Winnie began to learn the names of the wild flowers which grew along the canal banks and in the meadows. There was a whole new world to explore! When she was looking after Clodhopper, it didn't seem like work at all because Winnie had grown to love the old horse so much and whispered all sorts of things into his ear as they travelled along.

As it was springtime she often saw lambs with their mothers skipping in the fields. It made her think about Psalm 23 and the other passages from the Bible which she read to Mabel and Dan most evenings. Since her fall into the lock they had read together the story in Luke chapter fifteen about the lost sheep. Sometimes they passed stone walls which formed a square and Mabel had told her that these were used as sheepfolds. The sheep were driven into the fold at certain times, so that their feet could be inspected and also the ewes when they were near their lambing time. It made Winnie think of the story of the shepherd leading his hundred sheep to the fold and counting them in. When he found there were only ninety-nine sheep, he realised that one had got lost. He settled the sheep and then went looking for the lost one. As she looked around the hills and dales of Lancashire, sometimes there were lots of brambles or deep ravines or craggy rocks, and Winnie thought it must have been hard to find the sheep. The story went on to say that the shepherd kept on looking until he found the lost sheep and carried it back to the fold on his shoulders. When he arrived back he called all his friends to come for a party, for he was so thrilled to have found his sheep.

Mabel had explained to her that people are often described as sheep in the Bible and that Jesus called himself the Good Shepherd. It was easy to decide not to bother about following him but go off and 'do your own thing', but by doing that you lose your way in life. However, if a person is sorry for disobeying God's commands and breaking his laws and tells Him so and asks Jesus to forgive him and come into his heart and life, it is like calling to the Good Shepherd to come and find you. He will always answer that prayer and in heaven there is much happiness because the lost sheep has been found and is back in the fold.

Winnie thought she understood what it meant but wasn't quite sure. She spent quite a lot of time thinking about these things as they went slowly on their way. There was plenty of time to think because the heavily laden barge struggled to make the maximum speed of four miles an hour down the canal.

As the weather became warmer, Winnie was allowed to sleep on the roof of the barge. She loved being under the stars and away from the smoky fire! Dan taught her the names of some of the stars and constellations. When she lived in the town there was always smoke from the factories and mills and often a thick fog so that she wasn't able to see the sky, let alone the stars. Winnie loved being out in the countryside. Everything would have been perfect except that she had no idea how Will was getting on and whether he had received her letters or when she might see him again.

One day Mabel brought her some more writing paper so that she could send another letter.

"Why don't you send it to the minister of the church?" she suggested. "Sometimes the workhouse Masters feel that their charges might be unsettled by letters from the outside world, but you said the minister was kind to the workhouse children."

"That's a good idea," Winnie replied. "I'll do that. I could write two letters, one to Will at the workhouse and another for the minister of St. Cuthbert's to give to him. That way Will should hear that I am safe and well."

It took Winnie the whole of a Sunday afternoon to write two letters in code to Will and another in English to the minister asking him to pass the letter to her brother. The next day, when they passed near a village, she took some coins from her wages pot and ran to the post office to buy stamps and post her letters.

Clodhopper was waiting for her when she got back to the canal. The boat was moored at a place called Igthehill and Winnie was a bit fearful about the next part of the journey—the Gannow tunnel. Could she manage to leg this tunnel? She talked to Clodhopper about her fears. He whinnied to her, but she knew he didn't really understand and couldn't talk to her or change the situation.

"How silly I am!" she said to herself. "I should be talking to Jesus. He can hear me and can help me!" So she stopped talking to the horse and prayed for help. Winnie so wanted to help her kind adopted grandparents but also was very, very scared!

Having prayed, Winnie jumped on to the narrow boat and went into the cabin. She was very surprised to find Mabel and Dan talking to a young man. She didn't know they were expecting a visitor. Maybe it was an official from the canal or coal company, she thought. Then suddenly another very horrible thought passed through her mind. Maybe it was a police detective trying to find her and take her back to The Cock and Hen!

"Come and meet our eldest boy," said Mabel with a big smile. "Sam, this is Winnie whom we were telling you about!"

Winnie shyly shook hands with the young man, relieved to know she was still safe.

"Well, Winnie," Sam said, "Ma and Pa have been telling me all about your adventures. I'm glad you're here to help them! However, would you mind if I legged the boat through the tunnel? I know it's not the longest (only 550 yards) but for old times' sake, I'd like to do it with Pa. It's ages since I legged through a tunnel!"

"Of course I don't mind. I'll lead Clodhopper up the towpath and through Barge Horse Lane to the other side," replied Winnie with a beaming smile. Dan winked at her and she had a funny feeling that he had had a hand in answering her prayer!

Winnie leapt off the barge, saying a quick 'thank you' to Jesus for helping her, and unhitched the old horse from the towpath and began to lead him through the lane. She knew she didn't have to hurry because the barge was heavily laden with coal and could only be taken through the tunnel very slowly.

Winnie and Clodhopper were soon through the lane and at the other end of the tunnel, but as there was no sign of the boat, she sat down on a stile by a field and admired the view. The large town of Burnley was left behind and in front of her was a lot of farm land.

As she was daydreaming, a gruff voice behind her made her jump off the stile. She turned around and saw an old man leaning on a stick. He was very well dressed. In Winnie's eyes he looked like someone very important.

"Good day to you, lassie," said the old man in his gruff voice. "Sorry, my dear, I didn't mean to startle you."

"That's alright, sir, I was just sitting and daydreaming, waiting for the barge to come out of the tunnel," she explained.

As she turned around, the old man began to stare at her, then as if he realised that he was being rude, he began to apologise.

"I'm so sorry, dear. I didn't mean to stare. You just look so like a little girl whom I knew many years ago. The likeness is quite startling, yes, quite startling!" he said, wiping a tear from his eye. "Please forgive me," he added, "but would you mind telling me your name?"

"It's Winifred Collins, sir, but most people call me 'Winnie' and a few call me 'Fred'," she answered.

He looked such a sad old man leaning on his stick and with a lovely golden retriever at his heels, that Winnie felt very sorry for him. She let go of Clodhopper's rope, knowing he wouldn't move an inch without her and climbed over the stile to stroke the dog.

"What is your dog's name?" Winnie asked.

"Goldie," answered the old man, "and she's very gentle. She will like being petted."

After a few moments, Winnie noticed something on the top of the old man's stick. It had a silver knob on which were entwined letters just like the letters on her mam's hanky. She was sure they were the same and kept looking at them.

"Sir?" she asked shyly. "What do those letters mean on your stick?"

"Ah, they are part of my family crest. My family goes back a long way and we have been squires in this area for generations. Everyone has names which start with the same letters, so the crest belongs to all of us," explained the old man to Winnie.

As he was explaining this, the narrow boat appeared from the tunnel and Winnie knew she must take Clodhopper to the towpath and hitch him up, but she so wanted to ask the old man something.

"I must go, sir," she explained, "but please, could you stay here for a little while. When Clodhopper is tied to the boat again, could I show you something my Mam gave me that's like your letters?"

"I'll wait a little while, dear," he replied. "It's so nice to talk to a young lady again!"

Chapter Sixteen

As soon as Clodhopper was secured to the boat, Winnie jumped on board and ran into the cabin.

"Hey ho! What's the great rush?" asked Dan. "We have time to stop and chat a little with Sam. Mabel is putting the kettle on for tea."

"Thank you, Dan," answered Winnie, "but first I just want to show that old man, who is the squire here, something which my Mam gave me. I think he might know what it means."

Quickly, she found her bundle and took the whole lot with her and rushed up the bank to the stile where the old man was waiting for her.

Very carefully Winnie untied her shawl and brought out the treasures in her tin.

First, she showed the old man her mam's hanky with the beautifully embroidered initials, E.M.E., all intertwined.

"It's just like your stick, isn't it?" Winnie said in excitement. "It belonged to my Mam and she gave it to me before she died. She gave me these too," continued Winnie, as she pulled out a pendant necklace and a brooch. "I also have the birth certificates for myself and my twin brother. Not everyone has birth certificates, do they? But we were born in 1854 after the law had been passed to register births," she added proudly.

The old man was in tears. However much he tried to stop them, they just would not stop pouring out of his eyes and down his cheeks.

"What is the matter, sir?" asked Winnie. "Have I said or done something to upset you?"

"No, my dear. Now I know of whom you remind me—it is your mother, Ernestina, my long lost daughter!" The old man took out a large pocket handkerchief and blew his nose.

"You see, Winnie, you are my granddaughter!"

Winnie was so amazed to learn this and longed to talk more with her newly-found grandfather, but Dan was calling from the boat and she knew she couldn't stay longer.

"Please, sir, Grandfather, I mean," she said, "that's Dan calling— he's my adopted Grandfather—we have to move the narrow boat on. If we are late getting the coal to its destination then he will be penalised and that's not fair. Could you climb over the stile and come with me to tell Dan and Mabel who you are so that we can arrange to meet again?"

Winnie helped the old man over the stile and with Goldie bounding at their heels, they made their way down to the barge. Winnie helped her grandfather on to the plank and into the narrow boat, which was then very crowded indeed since Sam was still there! Mabel hastily wiped the best chair and invited Grandfather to sit down and while she made another cup of tea he told the story of how his daughter had run away with Len Collins all those years ago.

"I was so stubborn and foolish," he told them. "I was too proud to write back when she wrote to me. I thought, 'She has made her bed and so now she can lie on it.' But deep down I hoped she might regret her decision and come home to me. She did write and tell me when the twins were born, but in my pride I tore up the letter and burnt it. Only a year or so ago I wanted to contact Tina and say how sorry I was that I had ignored her letters, but of course, having burnt them all, I had no address. I now find that I have left it too late. I can never say sorry to her. I so often have asked God to forgive my pride and unkindness and that one day I might find my family again, and I am just overwhelmed that he has answered my prayer this afternoon. I don't want to lose my granddaughter now that I have found her," the old man said, with great feeling.

Winnie looked at Mabel and Dan, who were quite speechless when they heard the whole story. They had been so kind to her, indeed, Dan had saved her life! She had grown to love them very much and didn't want to leave them to stay with a grandfather she didn't really know.

"I have promised to work for Dan and Mabel and help take this barge full of coal to Liverpool," she told her grandfather. "Then I'm not sure what I will do. I'm afraid to go back home and I'll tell you why in a minute, but I also want to be with Will again. Why don't I finish my agreement with dear Mabel and Dan and then come back with them to Gannow tunnel and come to visit you then. Perhaps, Grandfather, you could get Will out of the workhouse and allow him to visit you too. I don't know what Pa will say, but please, please don't tell him where I am."

"I would love to take you home with me now," said her grandfather, "but I do understand that you have agreed to work with these kind people until the load is delivered to Liverpool. I'll wait until you return, even though I know it takes weeks to work up and down the canal. Yes, of course I'll try to have your brother released from the workhouse. To think that my grandson is in a workhouse and that that would never have happened if I had forgiven my daughter and gone to find her! How sorry I am. I will try to make it up to you both now that I have found you!"

Grandfather realised that the narrow boat needed to be on its way to keep up with the schedule, so he thanked Mabel for the tea, and Winnie helped him off the boat. He gave her a hug and kiss and Winnie promised him that without fail she would return. He also wrote his name and address on a piece of paper.

"If you are in trouble at any time, write to me. If you need to come to me, take a train to Burnley and then a horse-drawn cab to the house. I will pay any expenses. If all goes well, when you come back here, climb over the stile and walk through the field. You will see the house ahead of you. It will be home for you whenever you need it."

Then the old man reached into his pocket and gave his granddaughter a gold coin—a sovereign! She had never seen one before and looked at it with astonishment.

"Take this, dear; you may need some money when you reach Liverpool. It's a big town. Make sure you stay in a safe place. Perhaps you will want some new clothes, for I'm sure all your hard work on the locks is making you grow!"

"Thank you so much," said Winnie and when she reached the cabin she put the coin in her wages tin. In her mind she planned to buy something really nice for Dan and Mabel.

After all that excitement, they were late leaving the tunnel to continue on to Hapton and then the halfway point of their journey, Clayton-le-Moors church, so Sam told his parents that he would stay with them for a couple of days and help them on their way.

"Thank you for promising to stay with us until we get back here," said Mabel to Winnie. "We love you as if you were our own grandchild. We will miss you so much when you do leave us!"

"That won't be for ages," said Winnie, "although I am thrilled to find my grandfather. It's like a fairy story, isn't it? If only Mam were still alive! Won't Will be surprised when Grandfather finds him! I think I'll write another letter to the minister and tell him about Grandfather!"

Life soon settled down again and Winnie continued to work her way along the Leeds and Liverpool canal, but every day she thought about her Grandfather and prayed for him not to feel lonely, asking God to bless him and keep him well.

Chapter Seventeen

Will was quite overcome when he arrived at the Rev. Franklin's house and was told that he would never have to return to the workhouse. So much had happened in such a short time that he was quite confused and it all seemed like a dream. His teacher, Mr Johns, tried to explain that when they had heard that he was to be apprenticed they had become very concerned for his well-being and made plans to help him.

"How would you like to become an assistant teacher?" Mr Johns asked him as they sat around the table eating the best food that Will had ever tasted.

"Rev. Franklin has a sister who runs a school in Skipton. It is growing fast and she needs someone to help teach the younger children. There is a place for you to stay if you don't mind sharing with the groom, a young lad called Jack. You will get food, accommodation and a regular salary. Then in the early evenings Miss Franklin will teach you, so that you can continue with your education and maybe one day you could go to university!"

"Do you really mean it?" asked Will. "It would be so amazing! I can't think of anything I'd rather do for a living. I so want to go on learning too. I just wish that Winnie was able to be there and go to school as well!"

"We'll see what we can do—but first of all, you need to get settled! Come, let me show you your bedroom, and you must count this as your home now and maybe come back for the school holidays," said the minister, leading Will up the stairs and into a lovely bedroom. It wasn't a huge room, but it had books on the shelves and some games and toys. Will had never slept anywhere as grand as this before!

"This was my son's bedroom, but he is a man now. He is in the army and serves in India. He is married and I have two granddaughters, which one day, I hope, I will have the joy of seeing," he added.

"Sleep well, Will, and tomorrow I will settle things at the workhouse for you. We need to go shopping to get you kitted out, and then I will take you to my sister's house for you to start your new life."

"Thank you, sir, thank you so much. I really don't know how to thank you properly," said Will. "Maybe God was looking after me after all. I wondered if He really cared when all these bad things happened, but in the cellar I prayed to Him and gave my life over to Him."

"He cares, Will. He loves each of us so much, and all our prayers are heard. That doesn't mean that bad things never happen, because there is so much evil in this world. However, when we give our lives to Jesus, He promises not only to hear and answer our prayers in the way which He knows is best for us, but He also promises never to leave or forsake us," answered the minister. "Off to sleep now and we'll talk more tomorrow. You have a big day ahead of you!"

It was a big day too. Rev. Franklin went out very early to sort things at the workhouse. When Matron gave him the bundle containing Will's few clothes and possessions, he felt very sad. The lad had so little. Then the minister was given papers to sign to say that he took all legal responsibility for Will until such time as he was an adult or his father returned from Australia and claimed him.

Next, Rev. Franklin went back to the vicarage and collected his now-legal ward, and they went shopping. The minister told Will that he needed a cabin trunk. Then there were clothes for night and day, new shoes, a lovely box of pencils and some writing paper. He was given towels and soap, hairbrush and comb and shoe polish and brushes. Never had Will had so many things. It was like a million birthdays and Christmases rolled into one! Then the minister even bought him some sweets! The last present was the very best of all. He bought him a leather Bible and a prayer book.

"Please try to find some time to read the Bible every day— maybe just a few verses, but something. I suggest you begin with the New Testament. You will find that easier than starting at Genesis," explained Rev. Franklin.

"I promise I will, and thank you so much," answered Will.

After a hearty lunch the minister called for the pony and trap and drove Will to his sister's home in Skipton. He felt like a king, riding in the trap. It was all so exciting. If only Winnie could see him now! His only sadness was that he didn't know where she was and also that he had left Eric behind. He quietly prayed for them both, that they too would be safe and happy.

School was ending by the time they arrived, and Miss Franklin welcomed Will as if he were her son rather than an employee. Will liked her. She had a 'smiley' face and a kind voice. He knew he would be happy living and working in this new place.

When he met Jack, the young groom with whom he was to share a bedroom, he knew instantly they would be friends. Jack had a cheerful grin and seemed pleased to show him around.

The next day Will began his working life. He had become used to helping the younger children in the workhouse, so he didn't find teaching at all difficult. When it was playtime, the little boys were so pleased because he played games with them in the meadow behind the house.

The days passed quickly. Will and Jack became good friends, though Jack couldn't understand why he liked going for classes with Miss Franklin after tea! However, Will loved those times and began to borrow lots of her books to read. She had started to teach him both Latin and Greek because she was sure he would one day gain a place at university.

On Saturday afternoons Will went to the vicarage to visit Rev. Franklin and stayed over for morning church and then Sunday dinner before he returned to Skipton. Will enjoyed those Sundays so much! He managed to see Eric and usually had a little chat with his friend. Mr Johns often was invited to join the vicarage family after the service for Sunday lunch, and Will told the two men what he had been learning through the week as well as some of the funny things which the children in his class said and did. After lunch they read the

Bible together and Rev. Franklin explained to Will what it meant to be a follower of Jesus and prayed with him before he left them for another week at school.

On one of these Sundays, Rev. Franklin gave him two letters to read. They were from Winnie! One was to him, all in code of course, because Winnie didn't know that he was now in a safe place with a good job! The other letter had been written to the minister and told him all about their grandfather. Will was amazed! He was so excited to learn he had a grandfather who wanted to meet him as well as hearing that Winnie was happy and well.

In fact, soon afterwards, his Grandfather arrived at the workhouse to try to find Will. The Master told him where Will had gone to work and also about his father having been deported to Australia for ten years of hard labour! Grandfather was then directed to the vicarage and met Rev. Franklin who told him in glowing terms what a lovely young man his grandson was and how he was working and studying very hard. Then even though it was the middle of the week, the minister took the twins' grandfather in his trap to Skipton to meet Will.

Will was so excited to meet his grandfather and heard all about Winnie and her adventures. Grandfather promised that as soon as Winnie came back from Liverpool to visit him, then he would come and collect Will and they could all be together and live as a family.

"Of course," Grandfather said, "I shall send you both to good schools so that you can finish your education, but we'll have lots of fun together and make up for all the years we have missed!"

It was quite hard for Will to settle down again and work hard after his grandfather left with Rev. Franklin. He had no idea how long it would be before Winnie arrived back at their Grandfather's house, but he knew it would take a little while as canal boats went very slow. He tried to be patient and each day thanked God so much for all He had done and for changing his life like He had. He also prayed for his family; for Winnie to be kept safe; for Grandfather that he would stay well and strong; and for his father that wherever he was, on the high seas or in Australia, that he would also come to know the forgiveness of God and find peace and comfort.

So the spring passed and the days became longer as summer progressed. Winnie's journey to Liverpool went very well. Dan and Mabel took great care of her when they reached the big city, and how glad she was that they did. Winnie had never seen such a huge place, full of people bustling around. She would have been very frightened if she had been on her own. From her savings and the sale of her two long plaits, she was able to buy some presents, something nice for Dan and Mabel, for Will and for her grandfather. Then Mabel took her to a large shop and she bought some clothes with the sovereign which her Grandfather had given her, ready for the time when she would live with him. How she longed for that day and to see Will again! As she prayed for all her family, she too thanked God for all the blessings he had given her and that he was her Good Shepherd and she was one of His flock, safely in the fold.